40p

MISLEADING ENCOUNTER

Willow Cavendish had good reason to dislike Ryden Kilbane and yet she found herself falling in love with him . . . and that made his hatred of her, however misguided, so much harder to bear.

Books you will enjoy
by JESSICA STEELE

NO HOLDS BARRED

Zare Forturini saw Laine as nothing but a gold-digger. Only it wasn't his money that Laine was attracted to, but the man himself. Couldn't he see that?

NO HONOURABLE COMPROMISE

When Holt Jepherson got the seat on her father's board that she had thought was rightfully hers, Verity was furious and vowed revenge. Then she had an idea. What was wrong with seducing Holt and then compromising him? Quite a lot, as it turned out . . .

A PROMISE TO DISHONOUR

Ashlie knew she was immune to the charms of rakes like Chase Marriner. Could she prevent her sister-in-law from falling under his spell by distracting Chase herself?

MISLEADING ENCOUNTER

BY

JESSICA STEELE

MILLS & BOON LIMITED
15–16 BROOK'S MEWS
LONDON W1A 1DR

First published in Great Britain 1986
by Mills & Boon Limited

This edition 1986

ISBN 0 263 75340 9

Set in Monophoto Times 10 on 11 pt.
01–0486 – 57652

Made and printed in Great Britain by
Richard Clay (The Chaucer Press) Ltd,
Bungay, Suffolk

CHAPTER ONE

AT first light, Willow opened her eyes to observe that the heavy rain of the night had given way to a fine drizzle. Convenient excuses to turn her back on her new pursuit of an early morning jog were readily available. The weather conditions were against it for a start, and nobody in their right mind was astir at this hour. Besides which, this *was*, after all, the first day of her holiday. Not that she was going anywhere. Not that she could afford to go anywhere *now*.

Willow shrugged off all thoughts on the state of her finances and, closing her eyes, prepared to snuggle down for another half an hour or so.

But only to have her conscience nag that for a twenty-one-year old who had, through force of circumstances a month ago, decided to be more outgoing—this wasn't the way it was supposed to go.

Ten minutes later, dressed in a pink tracksuit, she pulled the door of her cottage to, and set off down the street, her mind coming more fully awake with every trainer-clad step she took.

She was glad she had made the effort as she jogged silently past houses that still had their curtains drawn against the night, and had started to enjoy the solitude of her run, when she reflected how at odds she must be within herself, that she should enjoy this early morning solitude, and yet, so often, since Mrs Gemmill had died, she had felt lonely.

A sadness for Mrs Gemmill's passing touched her, but she mused that it was natural in this period of adjustment, that she should miss the dear old lady who had been more like a mother to her than a landlady.

She jogged on, her thoughts straying back four years to just before she had moved in to live with their next-door neighbour. Mrs Gemmill had been in fairly good health then, and Willow had just left secretarial college to start work at Laffard Fine Porcelain. Her parents had long since divorced, and she lived with her mother, who was quite happy that they seldom saw the man who, up until then, had paid the rent and maintained them both.

Daphne Cavendish was an attractive woman, and occasionally some man or other would call to take her out. But, then Bruce Humphreys came home on leave from his job in Hong Kong and was suddenly always at their home. Her mother appeared quite girlish all of a sudden and Willow quickly realised that not only was he keen, but also he might want to take her mother with him on his return to Hong Kong and that her mother might want to go with him.

When her mother came home with Bruce's engagement ring on her finger, and told her they were shortly to be married, Willow found that any ideas that she too might have nursed about being Hong Kong bound, were groundless hopes, for although Daphne Cavendish had made plans for her, they were not in a Far East direction. It was soon apparent that, while Willow had been at her office learning the difference between what one was taught of office procedure at college and what actually went on in an office when one was thrown in at the deep end, her mother had taken advantage of her absence to have a lengthy discussion with their next-door neighbour.

She arrived home one night to find that everything had been settled. Her mother had led up to it by explaining that with the lease of the house about to expire, she did not intend to renew it.

'You'll hardly want accommodation here and in Hong Kong,' Willow had agreed: the notion that she would be making her home with her mother and Bruce having been encouraged by what had so far been said.

'I'm glad you see it like that,' Daphne Cavendish had smiled. That smile was still there when she had dropped her bombshell, and told her how Mrs Gemmill had agreed to take her as a paying guest.

'You've—arranged for me to live with *Mrs Gemmill*!' Several emotions had made themselves felt within Willow all at the same time—she was shattered to say the least. 'Why can't I stay here, in this house?' she had argued as she had striven to accept that quite clearly her mother had no room for her in her new marriage, and that it looked as though she was to be made to live with a lady whom, though a dear soul, to Willow's seventeen years appeared extremely elderly.

'I've just explained why. I'm giving up the tenancy of this house. Besides which,' her mother had stated, 'I don't like the idea of you living on your own.'

'I'll be all right,' Willow continued to argue, finding little comfort in the thought that her mother was not abandoning her totally without concern for her welfare. 'I can——'

'Anyway,' her mother interrupted, 'even if the agents would permit a seventeen-year-old to sign a fresh tenancy agreement, which I doubt, with the allowance from your father discontinued now you've started work, you'd never be able to afford the rental on your salary.'

The truth of that had hit home. As yet, her earnings were low and commensurate with her being on the bottom rung of her career ladder. It was then though, that a stubborn streak in Willow had asserted itself. The very next day she rang round all the agents to enquire what sort of rent she would be expected to pay should they have a vacant flat on their books.

It was galling to have to admit defeat when her vision of being a career girl with a flat of her own went up in smoke. For even the rent of the smallest flat, she had discovered, was way above her means.

So, Willow reflected, as she jogged past the Bell and Anchor and headed for the sacrosanct village green, her mother had married Bruce Humphreys and had gone with him to Hong Kong—and she had moved in with Mrs Gemmill.

But if early on in her tenancy she had had private thoughts that once her salary had risen to a sufficient level for her to be able to afford that tiny flat, they had soon started to fade when Mrs Gemmill, so mentally alert, had proved to be every bit as lovable as she had seemed. In no time Willow had forgotten the gap in their years, and by the time her salary had increased, the idea of moving out had long since gone from her mind. Instead, when Mrs Gemmill's legs had started to 'play up', Willow had bought a car, and the two of them had enjoyed many a drive.

Though it was that self-same car, Willow mused, as the village green came within sight, that was responsible for her present impoverished state. Last Friday, only the day before her car had been meant to take her away on holiday, it had packed up on her. She had promised herself that holiday too, for though willingly, unstintingly, she had given of herself to look after Mrs Gemmill when her health had started to fail, Willow had felt worn from broken nights, and emotionally exhausted from the constant fear that the dear soul might not make it through another day.

Never again would Willow want to live through that time when fear had become a fact, and Mrs Gemmill had died. Nor did Willow wish to dwell on how the relatives, never seen before, had descended within hours of Mrs Gemmill breathing her last, to claim whatever was going.

Willow turned her thoughts to how, sickened by all the rapacity that had gone on, she had wanted to move out with all speed. She had not immediately accepted the agents' offer of a very small cottage in Surrey, just over the borders of Hampshire where she lived. The idea of a twenty-mile drive to and from her place of work had little appeal, but, maybe because she had felt a little desperate, she had gone to see the cottage anyway.

Once seen, however, the charm of the old world village of Stanton Verney had so delighted her, that in no time the thought of the travelling involved each day had seemed a small price to pay to be able to live there.

It had taken almost all her savings to move into the cottage, for not only had there been furniture to buy, but sundry small items had simply run away with pounds. It was fortunate that she had kept a little money back for that much-needed holiday. So much for her holiday now.

The estimate for the unexpected repairs to her car—something to do with the differential unit according to the man from the village garage—was colossal, and would, as near as made no difference, clear her out.

With her car, or lack of it since it was not going to be ready before tomorrow, Tuesday, occupying space in her thoughts, Willow reached the village green. She would do just one circuit, and then go home and get out of her damp things and into a nice hot bath.

Although her residence in the delightful village of Stanton Verney was of less than a month's duration, it had been long enough for her to be acquainted with the existence of a zealous village green preservation society. For this reason, careful that not one blade of grass should know the smallest pressure from her slender frame, Willow kept to the tarmac surround.

Her thoughts drifted on to how, when her car had come to a full stop and she had needed a push into the side of the road, a couple of punks had come to her aid. A smile sweetly curved her mouth when she thought of the green-haired individuals who had assisted her. Then the memory of how one of the punks had sported a tail-coat over his jeans, faded instantly. Before her incredulous eyes, she distinctly saw that someone—someone who had obviously never heard of the Stanton Verney Village Green Preservation Society—had parked their car slap bang in the middle of the green!

With visions of the owner of the car being set upon by a lynching party if it was not moved before the village awakened, Willow padded nearer.

It got worse! The nearer she came to the vehicle, the more clearly could she pick out that the tyres had churned up the grass! All too plainly the car had spun off the road while taking the turn, and had skidded to a halt.

Oh grief, she thought, somebody's for it! It was then, as her eyes left the tyre marks, that her glance was drawn to the inside of the car. Abruptly, she halted. There was a male body slumped over the steering wheel!

Her eyes still glued to the lifeless body that moved not a muscle, Willow stepped over to the driver's door and peered in through the window.

She strove hard to hold back her imagination which ran riot when she could detect no sign of life in the fair-haired man. There was no sign of any accident that she could see, nor the smallest hint that the man was breathing. She could not help but wonder—had he chosen the village green of Stanton Verney as a suitable place to commit . . . suicide!

Fearing that this might be the case, Willow raised a

hand to bang hard on the glass. But when that brought forth no response, she saw there was nothing for it but to open the car door and to hope that he would not fall out, stone cold dead, at her feet.

With her hand already on the door handle, suddenly her anxious eyes noticed two things almost simultaneously. One, there appeared to be a flicker of movement from the sweater clad arm, the other . . . on the passenger seat beside him, lay an empty scotch bottle.

A drunk! He was drunk! He wasn't dead—but merely the worse for drink!

Relief poured through Willow as she took a step back. She had been ready to play her part in calling out the necessary services had the man been the victim of natural causes, or suicide. And if he had been merely ill, she would have rendered what assistance she could. But, when his other arm moved, and it appeared he was coming round from his drunken stupor, she decided that the man could manage quite well on his own. She left him to his own devices.

But, on her way to complete her circuit before she headed back to her cottage, Willow found that although able to leave the man to come round in his own good time, she could not shelve a niggle of apprehension about how long his recovery would take.

Her imagination began to take off again when she considered that soon the whole village would be astir—if someone wasn't out and about already! She remembered those deeply grooved skid marks made by the drunk's car, and grew afraid that, when there was hell to pay apparently if anyone so much as dropped a toffee paper on the village green, the village green guardians would have the police there breathalysing him before he was conscious enough to say, 'Blow into what bag?'

Willow finished her single circuit of the green, and then decided that she would break with her usual practice, and would do a second circuit.

Her imagination on that second circuit saw the fair-haired man as a young man who'd had a row with his wife, but who, if breathalysed, would surely, the state he was in, lose his licence. He probably had a couple of children too.

Willow glanced over to the car to observe from the registration number that the car was less than a year old. Which had to mean, she considered, he had a fairly good income. Which in turn meant, she decided, since in her own case it was essential for her to have a car to get to work, that if the young man did lose his licence, he could well lose his job too.

With these thoughts plaguing her—of the man still slumped over the steering wheel losing his livelihood, and how the security of his family was going to suffer for it—Willow again came to a halt near the car.

Not certain then what to do, or indeed, if she ought to do anything, she stood there indecisively. Then suddenly the memory came of how when she had been in distress and in trouble with her car, only last Friday, two punks had come to her rescue. They, she clearly recalled, had, despite appearances, been really super. She had been glad of their help. So—what did appearances matter? Those youths had been kindness itself.

With the thought, so what did it matter if the man behind the wheel was a chronic alcoholic—there was a kindness here that had to be passed on, Willow quickly moved. Time seemed of the essence as she hurried to open the driver's door.

The stench of stale alcohol nearly knocked her back, but try as she might as she grabbed hold of a handful of sweater and shook the man, and sharply instructed, 'Wake up!' he would not.

There was life there though. Anxiety mounted within her in case they were both still there when the avengers arrived to hang, draw and quarter him. Then she saw what she had to do. She was glad to have some assistance from him, however minimal, when he seemed to get the general idea that she wanted him to move over.

With the bit between her teeth, Willow pushed and shoved, refusing to listen to an inner voice that told her to leave him where he was to take what was coming. She had been helped on Friday, it was his turn now.

She felt near to exhaustion when, at last, the man was sufficiently clear of the gear lever for her to do something about getting him and his car out of there. Luck was with her when, with the engine ticking over, she found that the car was not so deeply embedded in the mud patch it had made of that particular part of the green, that she could not move it.

Very slowly she reversed the car. Once on the tarmacadam though, she lost no time. It was meant to be, she mused when, having considered various alternatives, she realised that the obvious place to take her cargo was back to her own cottage. It was meant to be . . . why else was the garage, that usually housed her car, empty?

Before she hid his car away in the converted outhouse though, Willow realised that it would be simpler to get her 'guest' inside her cottage first. This proved to be easier than she had thought, for whether because of the motion of the car, or whatever, the fair haired man had come sufficiently out of his stupor to open a pair of glazed, bloodshot eyes. Though as yet incapable of talking, there did seem to be some life in his grey matter for he seemed to comprehend that she wanted him on his feet, and walking.

With unsteady gait, Willow propelled him indoors,

and left him collapsed on her settee staying only to push a cushion under his head. Then she hastened to open up the garage and tuck his car out of sight.

He was dead to the world when she went back in to the cottage and she decided he would come to no harm if she left him again. Willow raced upstairs to have the quickest bath on record and to rub the dampness from her long blonde hair. Though she was not absent for long, by the time she went downstairs again, her guest had shifted from his recumbent position, and was now more sitting than lying, his bloodshot eyes open and on her as she came into the room.

'In answer to your first question,' she told him when he appeared to still not have the energy to talk, 'you're in a cottage in Stanton Verney, and you've just been rescued from a fate worse than death.'

The flicker of recognition at the name Stanton Verney suggested that, though Willow could not recall having seen the man before, he could quite well live locally.

'Do you live around here?' she asked. It seemed he could not remember where he lived, for he did not reply. 'I'm Willow Cavendish, by the way,' she smiled, and taking a step toward the kitchen, 'I'll make you some coffee.'

She was almost through the kitchen door, when a cracked, though cultured, voice asked, 'Have you—any—aspirin?'

Willow dissolved a couple of aspirin in water and took them to him. She closed her eyes to the shaky hold he had on the glass, and returned to the kitchen to put the kettle on to boil. Black coffee seemed an obvious prescription. Deciding to join him in a cup, Willow collected milk from the stone slab within the walk-in larder and reflected that—she had more time to think on other matters now that her guest looked to be coming round more and more by the minute—the refrigerator she had promised would be her next purchase, would have to wait until her bank account had recovered from the cost of her car repair.

Her guest had again shifted his position when she took the coffee in. And the liquid containing the soluble aspirin had taken the cracked note from his voice, she noted when, as if she had only just asked the question of, 'Do you live around here?' he informed her, 'The family home is in Comberford.'

Comberford was a village about seven miles away, Willow recollected as she handed him his coffee. Struck by the dreadfully unhappy look of him—not that she expected him to look full of the joys of spring with the kind of hangover he must have—she tried to tease a smile from him with the dry comment, 'You nearly made it.' But there was no answering smile to be drawn.

He appeared to be a harmless enough man, somewhere in his mid-twenties, she thought. Willow sat and watched him as he took a long draught from his coffee cup and, any movement painful, winced. 'God—my head!'

'The aspirin will soon start to work,' said Willow sympathetically. 'Though it's not surprising you're feeling a little—fragile—if that bottle was full when you started.' His eyes focused on her in a blank stare. 'There was an empty Scotch bottle on the seat beside you,' she explained.

He eyed her solemnly for a few moments. 'Where was I?' he roused himself to ask.

'In your car—which was on the village green. The village green,' she thought she should mention, 'is hallowed ground. You'd—er—churned it up a bit. The Village Green Preservation Society would have lashed you to a ducking stool, if they'd been first to come across you.'

'Hence a fate worse than death?' he mumbled. She saw thus, the first real signs of life and intelligence. She nodded, and he finished the remains of his coffee in one go. 'Any more?' he asked, and passed his cup over to her.

A half an hour later, more life and more intelligence had come through. But the young man, whose name she had learned was Noel Kilbane, still looked as sad and unhappy as he had earlier been. He thanked her for her rescue of him, and apologised for the condition she had found him in, and explained it was seldom that he went on a bender, but that he had needed a drink last night.

That he had taken more than one drink, and that he still had his problem with him on waking, was obvious. Willow could not help but feel sorry for him, but it sprung to her mind that his family over at Comberford would probably be going demented wondering why it was that he hadn't been home all night.

'If you'd like to ring your wife,' she suggested, pointing to the telephone, 'I can leave you to . . .'

'I'm not married—or ever likely to be,' he said flatly. And to her horror, a dreadful shuddering breath came from him, and his face twisted as though he was in torment from some inner grief. She thought he was going to burst into tears. He did not break down but manfully grabbed at some control. It was as if those words 'or ever likely to be' had released a tightly screwed down valve inside him, as though he could not bear the pain he felt any longer. Pained words were suddenly spewing from him, and Willow learned from every wounded syllable, the reason for his look of deep unhappiness.

Apparently, he and his girlfriend, whom he referred to only by the nickname of Gypsy, had just spent the most fantastic weekend together. So fantastic had it been that when, on finding her flatmate out when he had returned Gypsy to her flat in Crawley, he had thought everything was all in favour of his asking Gypsy to marry him. He'd been wrong. He had been shattered when she had turned him down and, unable to accept no for an answer, had, so Gypsy had told him, 'badgered away' at her until they had ended up having the most God-awful row.

'I'm so sorry,' Willow murmured gently, able to see for herself that it had not lightened any of his heartache to relive what had happened. But with the cause of his being unconscious through drink, now out in the open, she added 'You obviously felt in need of a drink when you left her.'

'I only meant to have one,' he said. 'But I was so stewed up, that one wasn't enough—there are scores of pubs in between Crawley and Comberford. I was still stewed up at closing time—I bought a bottle on my way out of the last pub I called at. As you know, I never made it to Comberford. It wasn't until the car went into a skid I should have been able to control with ease, that, when I did manage to brake, I realised that not only shouldn't I be driving, but I was also in no state I should like my parents to see. My father,' he went on to explain, 'suffered a stroke a few months ago. Ryden has impressed on me that nothing must be allowed to upset the old chap. Anyway, I can remember little after that except for thinking that I might as well stay where I was since I wasn't going to go to sleep if I did go home. I suppose I must have finished the bottle off,' he said, a haunted look in his eyes, his head again obviously filled with thoughts of his ex-girlfriend. 'I must have flaked out.'

He ran out of words then, and fell silent. But, since his pain seemed to have dimmed when he had been talking of people other than Gypsy, Willow felt a sympathetic urge to direct his thoughts into other channels.

'Is Ryden your father's doctor?' she asked. •

Noel shook his head and winced. The aspirin had obviously not found its way to the whole of his skull. 'Ryden's my brother,' he told her, a proud light coming to his eyes. 'He's in the States at the moment,' he added. But it was plain that Gypsy was never very far from the forefront of his mind, for that look of hopelessness was back in his eyes. He went on, 'It wasn't until Gypsy and I were in the middle of a furious row, when she flung at me that if she was going to marry anyone it certainly wasn't going to be any *mere* junior partner, that I realised I must have sung my brother's praises much too often. I've not had chance yet to introduce her to any of my family, but even so she's apparently far more impressed with Ry, than she is with me.'

By the sound of it, the row had indeed been a furious one, but again Willow was of the view that Noel's pain might be eased if she got him away from thoughts of Gipsy.

'You're a junior partner in some firm?' she asked.

'Kilbane Electronics,' he answered. Willow recalled that she had heard of the firm who were said to be one of the leaders in a very competitive world of micro-computers. Noel, all his thoughts clearly leading straight back to his ex-girlfriend, was, meanwhile, still talking. 'I told Gypsy that I might be only the junior partner, but I wasn't so hard up that I could not amply provide for a wife. But she threw back at me—when I know damned well I'm good at my job—that it's only because I was the brother of the boss, that I'd got the marketing manager's job in the first place.'

Oh dear, though Willow, they must have gone at it hammer and tongs. 'I don't suppose she meant it,' she tried to soothe. 'One cross word often leads to another in heated argument.' And still attempting to take the soul-tormented look from him, 'I expect Gypsy is regretting this morning that she said half of the things she did.'

'I wish I could believe that,' Noel replied despondently. 'But I can still hear her screeching at me as we parted, that I'd been so immature as to take all the fun out of our relationship and not only did she never wish to see me again, but also when she did marry, it would be to a senior partner, or nothing.'

Willow was not sure then what to say. It was obvious that she was wasting her time in trying to get his thoughts away from his hurt, and away from his ex-girlfriend. But then, all at once, whether because his head was starting to clear, or from whatever cause, there was suddenly a slightly self-ashamed expression coming to his face. And just as suddenly, there was a hint too of the smile she had given up hoping to coax from him, when he said:

'God, you must think me the wettest article since drip-dry was invented!'

'Not at all,' she protested quickly. They were ships that passed in the night and if it had been of some small help to him that she had sat and listened to his outpourings, then she had two weeks stretching in front with nothing else to do.

'I don't usually go on like that,' he apologised. He tried to find another hint of a smile, 'It's usually Ryden's ear I bend with my troubles, but . . .'

'But your brother's out of the country,' she smiled encouragingly. That did not seem to be enough for Noel's smile did not make it. 'Think nothing of it,' she assured him. 'Anyway, I was expecting a rather uneventful day, so you could say that you've taken my mind off my own troubles.'

'You're having trouble with *your* love life?'

Her love life was non-existent. When Mrs Gemmill's health had started to deteriorate, there had been more call on her spare time at home. None of Willow's boyfriends had meant anything very much, so it had been no hardship to decline invitations out in favour of doing what she could to comfort the dear lady of whom she had grown so fond.

Willow shook her head. 'I'm having trouble with my car,' she explained, and went on to tell him how her car came to be in the village garage until tomorrow, ending, '. . . so you have to thank a couple of punks, that I decided to pass a kindness on, rather than leave you to the untender mercies of the village green committee.'

At long last, Noel's smile did show through as he opined that he didn't think he had been in any condition to put up any resistance if they had set about skinning him alive. 'Where did you put my car, by the way?' he thought to ask. 'What brain I've got at the moment, tells me you haven't left it parked outside.'

'It's hidden away in my garage,' Willow grinned, and left her chair to collect the car keys from where she had dropped them down on the bookcase. 'You look more able to drive now, than you did,' she said as she handed them to him.

'I've taken up too much of your time,' said Noel, obviously reading her remark as a hint that he should go.

'No you haven't,' she denied. 'This is the first day of my holiday from my job, so I've nothing to rush round for.' She resumed her seat to confirm she had not been giving him a broad hint to go, only to see a frown crease his brow, as talk of work this time, impinged on him. He glanced to his watch.

'Oh Lord,' he groaned, 'I'm supposed to be airborne!'

'You've a flight booked?' Willow asked. 'You're on holiday too?'

'No such luck,' he replied. 'There's a computer show opening in Paris tomorrow, I'm supposed to be doing my stint there for all of this week, and to stay on to have discussions with one of our most valued clients the week after. No problem,' he continued a moment later. 'I can just as easily take an afternoon flight. It won't take long to drive to Broadhurst Hall, take a look at the parents, and get a bag packed. As long as I'm there for the opening tomorrow . . .' His voice tailed off, and Willow, observing that the look of pain was back in his eyes, guessed that his thoughts were again on his ex-girlfriend.

'Have you time to stay for another coffee, before you get off?' she quickly asked, though privately of the view that he must be awash with coffee. She thus attempted to give him something else on which to concentrate his thoughts.

As she had hoped, he came back to her. 'I'm sorry,' he apologised. 'Thinking about the show reminded me that it was at a show—nothing to do with electronics—that I met Gypsy. She does agency work,' he went on. 'I saw her on one of the stands. Having seen her, I forgot entirely what product she was promoting, I just had to go and speak to her.'

'Perhaps it will all come right,' she murmured, though she knew Noel did not have any hope of that.

But he had come a long way from the way he had been when she had first come across him, and was making great strides to be more in charge of himself. The next time he spoke, he rose above his need to talk about his lost beloved, and surprised Willow by latching onto something she herself had said.

'So,' he mentally shook himself, 'where have you chosen to spend your holiday—you get your car back tomorrow, I think you said?'

'I get my car back tomorrow, agreed,' Willow replied. 'But I shall be holidaying in Stanton Verney.' Still thinking that they were ships that passed in the night and with Noel having been so open, she saw no reason not to briefly explain that financially, she had just not been ready for such a colossal car repair bill. 'So bang goes any idea I might have had to have a change of scene for a few days,' she said, making light of it. 'Though with the weather turning out the way it has, I'd most likely come back from the coast more rust coloured than tanned.'

Noel smiled his commiseration. But, while he was fiddling with the car keys he still held in his hand, he seemed to halt in mid-thought to stare at the one key, in the bunch she had handed to him, that was obviously more of a door key, than a car key. Suddenly, he said urgently, 'Does your change of scene have to be at the coast?'

Nowhere near to guessing what was going through his mind, Willow answered, 'Not really. I just felt in the need to—recharge the batteries—to do something different.'

'Do you often get up to town?' he asked.

'London?' And at his nod she continued, 'I can't remember the last time——'

'Then it would be different, if you took your holiday there, wouldn't it?'

And before she had more than slowly agreed that perhaps it would, Noel separated the door key from the others on the ring, and told her, 'Ry and I have this flat in town where we lay our heads, most often, from Monday to Friday. Why not spend your holiday there?'

'I couldn't!' Willow gasped, not needing to think twice about it.

'Of course, you can. All you'll need is your petrol money. There's a freezer which, since neither Ry nor I are any good in the kitchen, is always well stocked with the goodies our housekeeper at Broadhurst plies us with every weekend.'

'But, I can't,' Willow tried to stop him. 'You barely know me. I barely know you . . .'

'That may be true,' he agreed. 'But you did save me from 'a fate worse than death' when, even though you didn't know me, you passed on a kindness. If the villagers had kicked up any sort of a rumpus, it would be bound to have made the local rag—which incidentally my parents take—and could have caused them anxiety which my brother and I would prefer they did not have. You saved me from that, too.'

Willow had not got round to thinking further than what the villagers might do to him. She was more glad than ever that she had 'rescued' Noel, when she recalled, with Mr Kilbane's recent stroke, how free from upset Noel had said his father should be.

'Please, Willow,' Noel tried to persuade, 'let me in turn, pass a kindness on. The flat's just waiting there to be used. And with Ryden not due back until the end of next week, and with me having no hope of returning to England until my discussions with Monsieur Ducret are completed, and they'll take the whole of next week, you'll have the flat entirely to yourself.'

The idea of spending a few days in London was, she had to admit, a new and exciting idea. But she had already told herself that they were only meant to be ships that passed in the night. Even if to take him up on his offer still meant that she would not see him ever again it wouldn't be right, so, it was only briefly that Willow hesitated.

'Thank you, but no,' she said firmly. And, hoping he would see that the subject was closed continued, 'I'll go and make that cup of coffee I promised you,' and, before she could weaken, went quickly to the kitchen.

She was grateful when she returned to the sitting room, that Noel did not refer again to his impulsive offer of the use of his London flat in his absence. Noel did not stay much longer. His coffee quickly disposed of, he then said that he had better get his skates on, or it would be an evening plane he would be catching.

Willow giggled when she let herself back into the cottage. Like a couple of thieves, she and Noel had furtively gone to her garage and got his car out of hiding.

That the unhappy young man had looked more cheerful on leaving than he had for most of the time he had spent in her sitting room, made her feel good too. As she automatically bent to pick up a cushion, that had somehow managed to fall over the back of the settee, so Willow saw the reason for Noel's cheery wave as he had roared off.

The crafty devil! Beneath the cushion, that had not fallen but had been placed on the floor where he knew she would see it, lay a key. With it, was a note written on a scrap of paper. With the key in one hand, Willow saw that Noel had written down a London address, and that he had also scribbled, obviously while she was in the kitchen making more coffee, 'Please accept. Kindnesses were made to be passed on.'

It was to be Wednesday evening before Willow made use of the key which Noel Kilbane had left behind, in spite of her initial reaction that it would be sent back to him at Broadhurst Hall, Comberford, in the very next post.

But she had delayed getting out her writing case. Her tidy nature refused to allow her to leave the cottage with the washing up not done. She was in the middle of rinsing through the cups and saucers they had used, when it came to her that since Noel would not be in

England to receive his mail for nearly two weeks, she had no need to rush out to the post box. A moment later, the disquieting thought arrived that, with an undoubted uproar going on in the village, she would invite a few uncomfortable moments if she ventured out and someone thought to ask if she knew anything about those deeply grooved tyre marks on the village green.

Thus it was then that the key was still in her possession on Tuesday. That morning, Willow did not need to look for an excuse not to don her track suit to take an early jog. It was not unlikely that some committee member had set their alarm to be abroad early and to watch to see who went by.

Housebound that day, as she had been the day before, a feeling of restlessness besieged Willow. More than ever did she miss old Mrs Gemmill. When Mrs Gemmill had been alive, there had always been some small task to keep Willow occupied, but now, with every single chore completed yesterday, time hung heavily on her hands.

Restlessness magnified into an urgent desire to be away and Willow grew more fed up than ever that her wretched car repair was going to take all of her holiday money. Fleetingly, the thought crossed her mind that if she wanted so desperately to have a few days away, then there was nothing to prevent her from using that key Noel had left behind. She batted the thought away. She would feel better when her car was returned.

Willow did not feel better when her car was back in her possession. She still felt a restlessness of spirit. Especially when an inner voice pestered that she had *promised* herself a holiday. Again, thoughts of that key invaded.

Noel had wanted her to use that key, that inner voice insisted, or why else would he go to the trouble to not only write her a note, but make sure she would find his note straight away? After all, no one left cushions lying around on the floor, did they?

She went to bed on Tuesday night and told herself she would feel better in the morning. At first light she opened her eyes and found her thoughts immediately straying to consider that, if she could not afford anything else, then she could afford London. All it would cost, would be the admittance fee to whatever sights she opted to see. Besides, she could take a look around any of the large London stores, without it costing her a penny, couldn't she? Again she ousted such thoughts. Only this time, such thoughts were much sooner back.

At five o'clock that evening, Willow gave in. Noel had insisted that she use the flat, hadn't he? He had really wanted to pass that kindness on, hadn't he?

Willow, after stopping to ask the way several times, eventually made it to the address Noel had written down. Then, with her car safely housed in the basement car park, she rode up in the lift and found the door that opened to the key she inserted.

Once inside the flat—it was entirely masculine and without frills—all her doubts and apprehensions about whether or not she was doing the right thing, disappeared. She was in London. She was on holiday. She was going to enjoy every moment of it.

Well, she would tomorrow. Tonight, she would settle in, have an early night, and be ready to take her fill of London from the moment she got up tomorrow.

There were two bedrooms in the flat, and Willow opted to take the one that had a dull looking tome on marketing by the bedside. This, she decided, since Noel was a marketing manager, must be his room. And since Noel had been the one to issue the invitation, she would not trespass into the personal room of his brother, the senior partner.

After a scratch meal of the few provisions she had brought with her, Willow tidied up and, intending to make an early start, laid the kitchen table ready for breakfast. Then, after wallowing for half an hour in a giant size bath, she got into bed and switched off the bedside light.

Warm in her bed, fed and bathed, she snuggled down contentedly. Her last waking thought was that she was on holiday, and how tomorrow, she was going to enjoy every moment of it.

For how long she had been fast away in contented sleep, she had no idea. But suddenly, some sound penetrated, and brought her rapidly to the surface. She listened hard, but all was silent.

Probably nothing more than noises usual to the apartment block, she mused. She relegated whatever sound it was that had disturbed her to nothing more than a normal sound to which her ears were not yet accustomed. Suddenly Willow sat bolt upright in her bed. Another sound had definitely occurred! It was the sound of someone moving about—inside the flat!

As alarm possessed every part of her, Willow was instantly certain that some miscreant, aware that the Kilbane brothers were both out of the country, was burglarising the flat!

Then, to her horror, before she could think what to do first, all of a sudden, and without ceremony, the door of the bedroom she occupied was suddenly pushed open. And, in the next moment, the centre light had been flicked on.

Shaken, her green eyes enormous, Willow sat and stared at the tall, dark-haired man who filled the doorway. With one eyebrow ascended heavenwards he, in turn, stood and surveyed her in her frilly nonsense of a nightdress.

Then while she was too petrified to let the thought

settle that this man looked too well dressed in his business suit to be some thief in the night, he finished his appraisal of her and her tousled blonde head. Not looking the slightest put out, he then casually drawled, 'Who do I find sleeping in my bed? Or, more to the point—who let you in, Goldilocks?'

CHAPTER TWO

HER eyes were still overlarge in her face, when what the man had just said broke through her fear. Relief rushed through her. By the sound of it, this was his home, therefore, he could not be an intruder. Willow lost sight of his question, and, through her confusion realised that she had selected the wrong bedroom.

'Am I—in your bed?' she asked, a huskiness in her voice which in view of the way her throat had felt parched by fright, did not surprise her.

Never once did his eyes leave her face. They were still on her when, taking his time, he coolly replied,

'No, actually—you're in the bed of my brother. But,' he went on in that same cool tone, 'the question still remains. How did you get in?'

More relief washed over her. This man was obviously Noel's brother, although according to Noel this man should at this moment be in the United States. If he was anything at all like his younger brother, he would understand when she explained everything to him. Not of course, that she could now stay on in the flat any longer than tomorrow.

'You must be Ryden!' she said, a smile of friendliness breaking now that fear and panic were gone.

His cool look was replaced by a grim-mouthed expression that told her he had taken exception to her claim to know him. Willow quickly realised that he did not share Noel's easy going personality.

'I'm sorry,' she apologised hurriedly. 'Noel said you weren't due back from the States until next week.'

Oh grief, she thought, when his reaction was to

positively glare at her, either she was telling this very badly, or her revelation that she knew his brother's name too, had not gone down very well. Again she rushed to explain.

'With Noel leaving for France . . . with both of you out of the country . . .' She halted, aware that in trying to get it all said at once, she was gabbling. She took a deep breath, then, more slowly, she resumed, 'Before Noel left my place to go to France . . .' She hesitated. A thunderous expression came to Ryden Kilbane's face, and that worried her. 'He said he was going to Broadhurst first—before he went to the airport,' she inserted hastily, in case that thunderous expression was on account of some belief that Noel had neglected his parents. 'Anyway,' she continued, 'I found the key to this flat after Noel had g . . .' She got no further, for his voice ripped through the air to cut her off.

'Of all the *bloody nerve*!'

Astonished, Willow just gaped. 'What . . .?' she began to ask, only to be even more astonished, not to say utterly flabbergasted, when once again she was explosively interrupted.

'I'll give you ten minutes to get your gear together,' he sliced ruthlessly in, his tone, his very look, brooking no argument.

Witlessly, she stared, unable to believe this turn of events, or that, incredibly, and at this time of the night, Ryden Kilbane seemed all set to toss her out on her ear!

'You don't understand,' she tried. 'Noel . . .'

'Not much, I don't,' he snarled, just as though he found his brother's name on her lips an insult. 'It's obvious you're in London to work some exhibition, just as it's obvious you don't live in London. But you can forget any idea to pocket your expenses while you use that key to take advantage of free board and lodgings until the show is over. The show, for you,' he ended threateningly, 'is over, right now.'

A blinding light of realisation that she had been mistaken for Noel's ex-girlfriend, started to shine. Willow was about to put Ryden Kilbane right straightaway, when her sudden discomfiture stopped her voice. If the rest of what he had said did not fit her, then that she was there taking advantage of free board and lodging certainly did fit. And, albeit that she was there by invitation, that discomfiture had her delaying a moment too long. She soon discovered that Ryden Kilbane was not prepared to give her a moment more in which to put him straight about anything!

In a few furious strides he had moved from the doorway, and long arms snaked down to tell her that in his opinion he had given her ample time in which to shift herself. Willow lost all thought to tell him that up until last Monday, she had never so much as clapped eyes on his brother.

Alarm again filled every part of her as firm hands clamped her arms, and the next she knew, was that she had been yanked bodily from her bed! Totally unprepared to be so unceremoniously manhandled, Willow had nowhere near got her sense of balance when, abruptly, Ryden Kilbane let go his hold on her.

Unable to do anything about it, she fell against him. In the short time she had known him she had been petrified and alarmed in turn, now she felt anger stir within her. Just as if the very feel of her body against his made him feel tainted, he roughly pushed her from him.

He proved quick off the mark for he gave her no chance to reply. Frustration mingled with her growing anger, for clearly he believed she had fallen against him on purpose.

Contemptuously he looked down to where her

breasts pushed at the material of her nightdress and, his tone insulting, he told her,

'*This* senior partner, has not the smallest interest in what's on offer.' And fixing her green eyes with a hard grey-eyed look, 'If you're not packed and dressed inside ten minutes, you'll go as you are.'

Her furious, 'Why you . . .' was met with the slam of the bedroom door. Having issued his instructions, Ryden Kilbane had left her to obey them.

Willow wasted thirty seconds of her ten minutes in laying her tongue to a few unpleasant names for the man who was not a man at all, but a monster. Nothing on God's earth would make her stay in the flat with him a minute after the ten he had allowed. She rushed to get some clothes on, and raced around getting her things together.

But, when five minutes of the allotted time had elapsed, so some of her anger with him faded. Several things became very clear to her then, the most obvious of which, was that somehow or other, the two brothers had spoken with each other since Noel had left her cottage on Monday. That crack about 'senior partner' confirmed it.

She then recalled how Noel had told her that it was usually Ryden's ear he bent with his troubles. Which could mean that Noel had told him even more than he had told her of how his fantastic weekend with Gypsy had ended with her scornful remark about her having no intention of marrying a *mere* junior partner.

Willow collected her hair brush from the dressing table and, remembering the pain that had been in Noel, began to understand why Ryden had been so furious. Noel had been bleeding inside with his hurt, and if any of his dreadful heartache had come through when he had been speaking with his brother . . . It was no wonder Ryden should feel outraged on coming home to the flat, to find that the girl who had treated his brother so heartlessly was, uninvited, making free use of it.

That Ryden had laid into the wrong girl, was a natural mistake, she saw too. Noel had told her himself that Gypsy had never met any of his family. Willow guessed that the unsocial hours Gypsy must work, could be responsible for that. Either that or, with Noel being so much in love, he had wanted to have Gypsy all to himself.

At any rate, it was as plain as day that Ryden Kilbane thought a great deal of his brother, and that anyone who upset Noel, would receive no mercy from Ryden. She did not have to look beyond the fact that she was being slung out in the small hours, to know that.

Willow retrieved her nightdress from the bed and pushed it inside her case, then closed the lid on her hurried packing. But, not liking that she had been mistaken for someone else, especially someone who sounded so hard hearted as Noel's Gypsy, she could not help but wonder if she could get through the granite exterior of Ryden Kilbane to tell him who she really was. For plainly, whatever conversation had passed between the brothers, Noel had still been too eaten up with his parting from Gypsy to remember, or to mention, that he had left the key to the flat with a girl who, for his own safety, had hijacked him and his car away from the village green at Stanton Verney.

At that point in her thoughts, the bedroom door was abruptly opened. And just one look at Ryden Kilbane's face, was enough to tell Willow that however much it rankled to be mistaken for some hard case who would settle for nothing but the boss man, she had lost her chance to tell him anything to the contrary. This glowering man did not intend to let her get a word in edgeways.

'Key!' he demanded, and held out his hand.

Willow dipped into her shoulder bag and wordlessly, she handed over the flat key. But impotent anger had her chin tilted that proud fraction higher when, her case in her hand, she stalked past him.

With pride on the march with her anger, she was half way across the sitting room, when she turned. Ryden had moved to the door which she knew was the other bedroom, so contemptuous of her was he, he was content to see her off the premises from where he stood.

'It's a great pity,' she began haughtily, 'that when Noel telephoned you in the States, that he did not tell you . . .'

'He didn't ring me, I rang him,' he curtly cut her off.

Uncivil brute, she dubbed him. Then a memory suddenly shot into her mind, of how Noel had said Ryden had impressed upon him not to cause his father any upset. Her anger dimmed. Her affection for Mrs Gemmill had made it instinctive in Willow to be caring of elderly people, and this evidence of Ryden's concern for his parents, had her momentarily side tracked, and unable to resist the question.

'You rang him to enquire how your father seemed when he saw h . . .' She broke off, the look of sheer rage that came to Ryden's face that such as she should dare to speak of his father, stopping her dead.

She knew then as she saw his hands suddenly clench, that Ryden Kilbane had had enough of her. And that was even before he barked aggressively, 'Out! Just keep your mouth shut—and get out.'

Willow wasted no more time. From the look of him, she did not give much to her chances of not being bodily ejected from the flat if she didn't get a move on. She had her hand on the door latch though, when pride demanded that she made some retort.

'I'm going,' she said tightly, dropping her case down when the security kind of lock proved a two handed job. 'Believe me,' she tossed angrily over her shoulder, 'it will give me the greatest of pleasure never to have to see you again.'

The door was open. All she had to do was to take up her case, and in the next second, she would be outside the flat. But—it all went badly wrong.

To start with, she was not to be permitted that second. Ryden Kilbane, obviously unable to wait to be rid of her, clearly thought he had done just that. He turned abruptly, entered his bedroom and snapped off the light switch. The sitting room was plunged into darkness and from that moment Willow was disoriented. She moved to take up her case. The slam of his bedroom door made her start, her shoulder bag fell down her arm, and somehow, in next to no time, she had stumbled, fallen over her case and, on her way down, had hit the door with a thud.

The outer door crashed to with such a din that would tell not only Ryden Kilbane, but very probably the whole apartment block, that someone had just, angrily, quit the flat.

But Willow had not gone—she was still inside the flat. As an agony of pain shot through her right leg though, she was completely unconcerned with what Ryden Kilbane, or anyone else, believed.

The cry that left her when she collapsed in a heap, had been lost beneath the din of the door slamming to. Willow did not cry out again, but as excruciating pain isolated itself to the area of her right knee, she knew that she was in trouble.

The agony increased when she attempted to stand to switch on the light to see what damage had been done. Indeed to stand, she discovered, was impossible. She had to bite her lip to prevent herself from crying out. Then she wondered if she had gone light headed, because she would have to cry out. She needed help.

She was about to call out and get Ryden Kilbane to come to her aid, when she remembered, all too clearly, his tough aggressive manner. Added to that was the memory that, regardless of the hour, he had not jibbed at throwing her out.

Willow's thoughts became confused when careless movement sent another spasm of agony washing over her. All she knew then, as she rode through to surface from pain, was that Ryden Kilbane was the last person she could ask for assistance. Somehow she was going to have to get to somewhere where there was light, so that she could examine the extent of the damage to her knee.

Not so much as a glimmer of light was to be seen from beneath Ryden Kilbane's door to show her the way. Willow, each movement beading her brow with perspiration, started to drag herself across the floor. Having said 'good riddance' to her, so he thought, Ryden Kilbane must be snoring his sublime head off in there. How she hated him.

All of her concentration needed to achieve the goal she had set herself, Willow put him out of her mind. She had to get to that bedroom she had used. There was a table lamp there. Surely she would be able to reach up and switch it on.

Never more had she needed her streak of stubbornness, as now. Stubbornness refused to allow her to give in as inch by tiny inch she edged her way over the distance that had taken only seconds the last time she had covered it.

A nightmare later she, with determined single-mindedness, at last achieved her goal, and light from the bedside lamp illuminated the room. Willow was too exhausted to do anything but slump against the bed. Bathed in perspiration, waves of faintness took her. It was, she realised, touch and go that she did not faint away altogether.

After some minutes though, the weakness passed, and she summoned up fresh energy to cope with the pain that she knew would come when she eased away her trouser leg. That her knee had already swollen was evident when Willow found she just could not roll her trouser leg up much further than above her calf.

Though she breathed more easily again when, with the trousers she had worn taken off and in a heap on the floor beside her, a quick examination of her knee showed that although it was swollen, there was no sign of a break.

Waves of faintness attacked again when, in need to find physical comfort, Willow dragged herself from the floor and onto the bed. So very nearly then did she call out to the man in the next door room. He was just going to love it, wasn't he, if, roused from a jet lagged sleep—and she reckoned she could assume he had only recently flown in from the States—he found she was still there. And he was going to love it even more when he saw that since there was no way she was going to be able walk unaided, let alone drive her car, if he wanted her out of the flat, he was going to have to drive her back to Stanton Verney.

The few hours remaining of that night, were the most terrible Willow could ever remember. She knew a cold compress might work wonders, but the idea of dragging herself anywhere beyond the bedroom, was beyond her.

With every movement an agony, she again shifted her position. But, whether from exhaustion or faintness, as dawn crept through the night sky, so sleep, in two minute snatches, drifted over her. Cold started to bite and Willow tentatively moved the bed covers over herself. She guessed she must be some state of shock, for the June temperature was mild. Again she drifted into a doze, but this time, it was for longer than just two minutes.

Twenty minutes later she was not sure if the pain in her knee had brought her awake, or if it was the sound of someone moving about in the room next door.

The sound of Ryden Kilbane's bedroom door being opened, had her searching for the best way to call out to tell him he still had company. Though since she had left her own bedroom door open she had no trouble, when she heard him roar, in realising that she had no need to tell him anything of the sort. He already knew!

She had forgotten entirely that her suitcase must still be by the outside door. The incredulous, 'She just *wouldn't* have the nerve!' swiftly followed by the appearance of the towelling robe clad figure who came striding in, reminded her she had left evidence of her non-departure lying around.

She had started to yell in fear even as his look of astonishment joined forces with an enraged bellow. But whatever it was she had screamed as he spared no time in reaching her, obviously had not penetrated. In a flash he had lifted her from between the covers and looked in no mind to put her down again until he had personally delivered her to the outside of the premises.

'My *knee*!' Willow screamed, agony like no other tearing her apart. 'I've hurt my knee!'

He favoured her with a despising glance that advised, even if her face was as pale as it felt, that he had no intention to be taken in by any ruse she had dreamed up. Then suddenly her lack of colour and the fact that she was not nightdress clad as she had been the last time he had yanked her from her bed, but was still wearing the shirt she had been wearing when he had thought he had seen the last of her, appeared to infiltrate his aggression, and he halted.

'I've sprained my knee,' Willow got in fast. And she was in so much agony then that, when Ryden Kilbane took his eyes from her face, she was beyond caring that all she had on below her shirt, were her briefs.

She saw his amazement when he flicked his gaze down the long length of her legs. For long moments all he did was stare as if not believing his eyes at the mighty swelling on her right knee. Willow felt her own aggression rise. If he ran true to form, the next she would hear would be an accusation that she had done it on purpose with the intention of furthering her acquaintance with the senior partner.

'How the——'

For once, Willow cut *him* off. 'It's all your fault,' she snapped, so unlike herself that she wondered if the pain she had endured had affected her normally sunny temperament. 'If you'd been less busy congratulating yourself on getting rid of me, you'd have waited to turn the light off, and I wouldn't have fallen over my suitcase.'

A murderous look was all the sympathy she received. Though she supposed she should be grateful for small mercies, in that when he moved with her back to the bed, he placed her down with far more care than he had lifted her from out of it.

But there was still nothing remotely resembling sympathy about him when, his tone accusing, as she knew it would be, he demanded, 'How the hell, with a knee like that, did you make if from the sitting room into this room?' And, his look as suspicious as the devil, 'Why,' he asked grimly, 'didn't you wake me?'

'In answer to your first question—with difficulty. In answer to your second, I'd got enough to cope with without waking you to breath more fire and brimstone that I'd been so inconsiderate as to dare to have an accident before I was off the premises.'

Quite suddenly then, she became conscious of her scant clothing. Aware of his eyes on her legs as he surveyed the result of her accident, she made a move to cover herself over. The scepticism that came to his hard eyes showed how much credence he placed on her modest and pushed more aggression to the surface.

'I can't stand, much less walk,' she flared angrily.

His sarcastic, 'That should keep you out of mischief for a while,' did nothing to lessen her aggression.

What did cause her rage to abate, however, was the fresh onslaught of pain that bit, when temper had her making a cross movement. Tears, weak tears, spurted to the surface. And for a horrified moment Willow thought, ironically, when she had endured grinding pain for hours without tears, that now, in front of this unsympathetic brute, she was going to do the unthinkable, and break down in front of him.

More aware than ever of him standing there considering what best to do with her, Willow fought a silent battle not to cry. Even so, having won that battle, her voice was snappy when she broke into his thoughts to ask, 'Does this establishment house any aspirin?'

'It hurts like hell, doesn't it?' he commented, flicking a glance to her pain worn eyes.

'That should please you,' she answered grumpily. She weathered another of his hard looks, and was snappy again when she asked, 'Well—does it?'

He moved from the bed, but not to go hunting up aspirin, for stopping on his way to the door to pick up the trousers she had so painfully struggled from in the small hours, he paused for long enough to drop them over a chair, and to tell her, 'This apartment block does house a consultant. You'd better see a doctor before you take any kind of medication.'

By then Willow was past caring who she saw so long as somebody would give her something to make the pain go away. Minutes ticked by when Ryden Kilbane left the room. She heard him speaking with someone on the 'phone, and more minutes ticked by. And the next time she saw her unwilling host, he had showered, shaved, and was dressed when he entered her room carrying, most unexpectedly, a tea tray.

'Sugar?' he enquired tersely.

Willow shook her head, and struggled to get into a position to accept the cup from him without slopping it over. He let her struggle unaided. She supposed that was because he knew just how much pain she was in and was feeling totally unsympathetic. But she knew better. She had seen his aversion that he'd had to touch her when ejecting her from his flat. He would not want to taint himself again if he could help it.

An impulse to try again to tell him that she was not his brother's ex-girlfriend surfaced. But, most oddly, when within the very next few seconds she was given a first class opportunity to do just that, Willow discovered that his treatment of her thus far, coupled with the agonising time she was going through, had established a contrariness in her nature she had not known that she possessed.

As he handed her the cup of tea and suggested, since the doctor would want to know whom he was treating, she had better tell him her name, the only thing she told him, was a sour, 'I thought you knew *everything*! Don't tell me there's something you've overlooked?'

He gave her a speaking look. But to her surprise, though probably not from any consideration for the pain she was in, he did not cut her down to size, but instead, curtly told her, 'I've only ever heard you referred to as Gypsy. I refuse,' he told her categorically, 'to call you by such an outlandish nickname.'

That he intended to call her anything at all, other than the names he must have silently called her, was another surprise.

'My name is Willow,' she told him tartly. 'But you can call me Miss Cavendish.'

Hostility between them was rife. The peal of the door bell announced that the doctor had arrived. Any vocal protest Willow had ready to tell Ryden Kilbane that she did not want him there while her injury was being examined, was not needed, for no sooner had he introduced Dr Oliphant, than he left the room.

Willow suffered more pain than ever when, in spite of his very gentle touch, the physician felt around the injured area. But he had a charming bedside manner and chatted away as though he had all the time in the world as he strapped up her injured limb, and concluded, 'You should mend.' While he put the bed clothes straight, he chatted on, his professional eyes taking note of the exhaustion in hers. Again he turned to busy himself with the contents of his case, the question appearing to be a careless one when he asked, 'Have you slept at all since it happened?'

'A little,' she replied.

'But not much,' smiled the portly man. He passed over a tablet, and said, 'Swallow that.' Willingly, she obliged, more than grateful that at last she had been given something to ease the pain. 'Two of these every four hours will keep you from feeling suicidal,' he then advised, and placed a phial of pain killers down on the bedside table.

Willow gave him her heartfelt thanks, and when he left her, she was in the happier state of knowing that the pill she had taken would soon begin to ease the pain.

Dr Oliphant had closed the door after him, but from the voices coming through the woodwork, she knew he had stopped to discuss the extent of her injury with Ryden. She was not totally surprised therefore, when, no doubt having heard that the swelling should go down in a couple of days, Ryden should come into her room toting her suitcase and shoulder bag.

A prickle of annoyance niggled through her gladness. Even if she did have to accept a favour from him in that he was going to deliver her to her home in Stanton Verney, there was no need for him to perversely place her belongings on the floor where she could not reach them!

'If you'll pass my case over,' she told him shortly, 'I can get a skirt to travel home in.'

His tight lipped look told her he was not overjoyed about her giving him orders. But neither was she overjoyed when, instead of passing her the case, he bent to open it and took it upon himself to personally search for the skirt she had asked for.

To her puzzlement though, he did not search at all, but did no more than extract the first garment to hand.

'I said, *skirt*,' Willow told him belligerently, in receipt of the garment he had just tossed to her. 'It is not my usual habit to travel in my nightdress,' she added for good sarcastic measure.

Her attempted sarcasm left him unmoved. Though even as she sensed something unpleasant was on its way, she was totally unprepared for his grim, 'You're not travelling anywhere. According to the medical bulletin, that knee needs forty-eight hours bed rest.'

She drew a horrified gasp—if her intelligence had got it right, her next forty-eight hours were to be spent in this flat—*with him.*

As if he was certain she was merely pretending to be horrified at the prospect, and that her injury had been most fortuitous from her point of view, Ryden snarled, 'You try to make capital out of this and with or without your night gear, I'll throw you out. Now, get the damned thing on, I've an office to go to.'

'I'll do no such thing,' she argued hotly. 'Dr Oliphant

has given me a pain killer—as soon as it starts to work I shall be leaving this flat, with or without your assist . . .'

'As soon as that pill starts to work, you'll be incapable of going anywhere,' he grunted. 'It wasn't a pain killer Oliphant gave you but, since in his opinion you need sleep, he gave you a . . .'

'A sleeping pill!' Willow gasped.

'He reckons it should knock you out for a good eight hours,' said Ryden Kilbane.

Defeated, suddenly all the fight went out of her. For the realisation was suddenly hers that, unless this brutish man intended to lug her sound asleep form around the country which, since he was more interested in getting to his office, he clearly did not, then she was stranded. She was totally at his mercy, and she had already painfully learned that mercy was something he held in very limited supply!

CHAPTER THREE

A THUMPING headache accompanied the nagging pain in her knee when Willow awakened that Thursday afternoon. She felt sluggish, had a dry mouth, and although she knew she must be rested after having been out for so long, she did not feel rested at all.

Gradually she came further and further out of the medication she had so innocently swallowed. Nevertheless, in need of something to relieve the ache in her knee and her head, she had no hesitation to reach for the pain killers the doctor had left for her.

As her hand hovered, and as her eyes caught sight of the water jug and glass which Ryden Kilbane had thought to leave for her, so her brain re-activated, and the short respite she'd had of a mind untroubled by thoughts of him, was over.

'Uncivil monster,' she muttered as the memory came flooding back of how he had indicated the 'phone beside her and told her she might like to make use of it to cancel whatever business she had on. How for one tiny second she had been crass enough to think that there must be a chink of kindness in him, she would never know.

The sleeping tablet she had taken must be responsible, she thought. For she had gone into the fantasy of thinking that there must be kindness buried somewhere beneath that concrete block he had for a heart. He had caught her wince of pain, when her nightdress had begun to slip from the bed and she had made an unthinking grab for it. He had come to retrieve it for her, and obviously assuming she was about to change into the nightdress, she had imagined a kindness in him that just wasn't there, when he had asked, 'Do you need help?'

She did not know any male that well that, whatever pain movement caused, she would allow that sort of help. Though it was without fuss, that she had quietly told him, 'I'll change when you've gone. But thank you just the same.'

Ryden had been bent over her, his hands ready to assist. In that moment of her quiet, dignified reply, he paused and, for once, he had looked at her with something more like puzzlement than aggression in the grey depths of his eyes. She had been so misled by what she thought was a hint of kindness showing through that, not wanting to be bad friends with anyone, she had felt a compulsion to put things right.

'About Noel and me,' she had charged in impulsively, only to see hard and instant aggression in the face that was so close to hers. Undaunted, she had tried to press on. 'My relationship with your brother . . .'

'I've heard the truth of *that* relationship, from Noel,' he had sliced through what she was trying to say.

'But you don't understand,' she persisted, 'it isn't . . .'

'You bet I understand,' Ryden told her cuttingly. 'You had ample time last night in which to concentrate your avaricious little mind on something other than the pain you were in.' He ignored that her green eyes were growing wider and wider at every snarled word he uttered. 'If you think I'd dream of believing one word of any tale that came off your lying tongue in preference to him, then you're showing yourself to be more simple than I know you to be.'

And leaving her with that to chew on, he had strode from the room, out from the flat and, she presumed, had gone off to his precious office. She had lain there fuming and wishing that she could make use of that 'phone to call someone, anyone, and ask them to come and collect her. But there was no one, and she had never felt so alone, or so miserable in her life. Sleep then, had been welcome.

The full glass of water which Willow swallowed with a couple of pain killers, coped adequately with her dry mouth. But when ten minutes later boredom set in, she was of a mind to test the strength of her right leg.

What seemed like an age after that decision, she had made it to the bathroom and sat on the bathroom stool, aware that she had not been too clever. If further trips to the bathroom were going to be the same staggering, lurching journey this trip had been, then it looked as though they were going to be very widely spaced.

More time was consumed when she transferred her weight and pushed and pulled until she had the stool over at the wash basin. From the mirror she saw that her face was without a scrap of colour and that her hair was a mess. She knew she would feel better when her skin had felt the touch of soap and water.

When finally Willow made it back to her bed, she was exhausted. Any notion there might have been when she had set out on her small adventure, that her injury might so rapidly have improved to allow her escape before Ryden Kilbane came home had been positively knocked out of her head.

She sighed in frustration, and railed silently against her fate. Then she remembered what a mess her hair looked, and caused herself more pain for she wouldn't settle until she had got out of bed to reclaim her shoulder bag. Not that she cared a hoot what she looked like when that monster returned, but it might make her feel better if she looked less of a wreck. When her hair was neatly combed, Willow could see no good reason why she should not apply a little powder and lipstick also.

To her surprise, Ryden Kilbane arrived home earlier than she had expected. Any mellowing thought that it might be on account of her that he had left his office early, was soon proved pure fantasy though. All of thirty minutes went by before he could bring himself to even look in on the invalid.

To Willow's way of thinking, she would just as soon he had not bothered, for it was plain from the start, that he had spent some of his day in re-energising his hatred of her presence there. She knew it the second he walked through the door.

He coolly observed her attempts to do something with herself, and for all the world as though he thought she had tarted herself up for his benefit. 'You managed to get out of bed, I see,' he said sourly.

The prickle of annoyance with which she was becoming, familiar in response to whenever he spoke, nipped at her again. She heartily wished she had not bothered with the morale booster of powder and lipstick.

'I'd have gone further than just the bathroom, if I could,' she told him scratchily. And not caring for his look of scepticism any better, she flared, 'Don't think I like it any more than you, that I'm virtually a prisoner in this room.'

'Of course you don't like it,' he taunted acidly. 'You must detest each dreadful second you're forced to endure—under the roof of the senior partner.'

Her temper rose. And it had nothing to do with Gipsy, or whatever other name Noel's ex-girlfriend went by. If Ryden Kilbane had not seen by now that she was nothing like the girl he thought her to be, then Willow was not of a mind then to pull punches herself.

'I wouldn't fancy you if you were the last man on earth,' she erupted angrily. 'From what I've . . .'

'Who said anything about fancying?' he chopped her

off icily. 'Though we both know you'd pretend to fancy the devil himself if he had the right kind of bank balance.'

She determined then, that never, ever, would she say another word to him, and Ryden, seeing he had effectively silenced her, strolled casually out again. Willow glared after him. Thank you, my knee is feeling much better, she silently mutinied. Too kind of you to enquire, but it hardly hurts at all, she fumed. Why he had bothered to enter the room at all, beat her, it certainly would not have worried him had she told him her leg had fallen off while she had been asleep.

She had no words to thank him when, presumably because he was having a cup of tea himself, he remembered her for long enough to bring her a cup too. Though, that he had thought of her at all, put a small dint in her rebellion. And when, an hour later, Ryden carried in a superbly cooked three course meal, even if most of the contents had come from the freezer, then with her starving frame fed, Willow was hard put to hang on to her mutiny.

Another hour went by and Ryden came in, looking terrific in a well cut dress suit, she had to admit, and deigned to ask did she need anything before he went out. She had so completely lost her mutinous feeling by then, that it seemed to her, utterly crazy that she should occupy a bed in the same flat and not tell him of the true facts about her short acquaintance with his brother.

'There's nothing I want, thank you,' she politely replied, as he picked up the tray of used crockery. Then, to delay him when she could see he had no time, or inclination, for a chat she blurted, 'My dinner was delicious. The home-made cooking . . .'

'I didn't . . .' he tersely started to cut in.

'Oh, I know it's the housekeeper at Broadhurst who keeps your freezer topped up,' said Willow quickly.

And hurrying on when she saw his brow come down that Noel, whom he thought she had treated so badly, must have told her that. 'Look Ryden,' she said, his first name slipping from her without thought, 'won't you please give me a minute to explain about Noel and me? Honestly you've got it . . .'

It was as far as she got. For to hear her speak his brother's name was apparently like waving a red rag before a bull. Abruptly he chopped her off, a fierce fury ablaze in his eyes as he slammed the tray down, and thundered: '*You* look.' Willow did not care at all for the aggressive jut of his jaw when he stated the way it was. 'In my haste to see the back of you, it appears I was too quick to assume you gone. And while it goes against the grain to admit liability for anything remotely connected with you, I've been forced, with you laid up, to accept responsibility for causing you to have an accident. But,' he continued to tear into her, 'if in accepting that responsibility I'm to be stuck with you, then—believe it—it's going to be played my way.'

'But I'm only trying to tell you——'

'Which means,' he hammered home, 'that if you don't want, *here* and *now*, to be pitched out into the communal hallway, then you'll keep to yourself whatever fairy tale you have to tell about the way you took all my brother heaped on you. You took his love, and led him to believe you returned it, only to screech out the truth at him, when he wouldn't take no for an answer, that you'd set your sights on someone who'd already made it to the top.'

Had Willow been guilty as accused, then when Ryden came to a furious stop, she would have felt shrivelled. But she was not guilty, and she was still determined to be heard.

'But Noel and . . .' Her voice faded when a look of totally enraged fury came to Ryden's eyes. As guiltless as she was, Willow shrank back in fear when, looking ready to tear her limb from limb, he took an ominous step forward. His voice was deadly, menacingly quiet. 'If you know what's good for you, you'll never mention the name Noel, in my hearing again. After the emotional battering you so uncaringly served him, it violates my ears to hear a bitch such as you so much as speak his name. So shut up,' he advised,—she did not feel capable of uttering another word—'and stay that way.'

Fifteen minutes after the flat door had closed after him, Willow had recovered from the real fear that just one more wrong word from her would have driven Ryden Kilbane to commit murder. His fury had been frightening, she admitted, and she had been truly scared. Having come away from her fear though, mutiny once again began to assert itself. Why should she explain how she and Noel barely knew each other? Hate for Ryden Kilbane consumed her, and had her damning him to hell that he had made such a scaredy-cat of her.

He had told her to shut up. Well, not another peep was he going to get out of her. *Particularly* on the subject of Noel. Everything came to those who wait, she thought, as her mind's eye took on the most delightful picture of one Ryden Kilbane coming 'cap in hand' to beg her forgiveness—she'd see him grovel first!

Sadly, the picture faded. For one thing, she could not see him grovelling to anyone. For another, since she was not to be allowed to tell him the truth, how else was he going to know that she had done nothing to deserve the treatment he dished out? It was certain he would not mention *her* name to the only other person who could tell him the truth, because whatever she thought about the brute, it had come over loud and clear that his love for his brother would not allow him to remind Noel of his hurt by making any mention of his ex-girlfriend.

She pondered for a while on the likelihood of something being said when Ryden handed Noel's key to the flat back to him. Then realised that Ryden would more than likely leave the key somewhere in the flat for Noel to find. Whereupon Noel, with his head still full of Gypsy, might give the girl who had rescued him from Stanton Verney village green brief thought, then pocket the key, and go back to have his mind consumed with thoughts of his ex-girlfriend.

Thoughts of the brothers Kilbane went from Willow's mind when, at half-past eleven, the pain in her knee began to drive her up the wall. She downed a couple of pain killers, but it was too soon for the tablets to work, and she found she could no longer stay in bed and just wish the pain away.

A good few minutes later she had struggled to the bathroom. She was consumed by a desire to ease the pain by removing the binding and applying a cold compress in the hope that it might afford some relief.

She was still in the bathroom and was in the act of renewing a wet flannel compress to her injury when, at midnight, she heard through the open bathroom door, that Ryden Kilbane had come home.

Bearing in mind that he had been as mad as hell with her when he had gone out, Willow calculated that it was most unlikely he would look in her bedroom to see how she was faring, and would, instead, go straight to bed. She carried on with what she was doing. She had no wish to see him again that night. For preference—not ever.

With her back bent and to the doorway, she all too soon had further evidence that this was not going to be her week. She heard his footfall nearby, and knew he had come to stand behind her. She tried to ignore him.

He was, however, difficult to ignore she discovered. Especially as none of his usual seething anger was evident when he enquired, 'Is the pain very bad?'

'At the risk of making you ecstatic—yes,' Willow tossed at him without raising her head. And since she did not care for an audience, she removed the compress, and began to rebind the swollen area.

'When did you last take your pain killers?'

Wishing him miles away she mumbled, 'Half an hour ago.' No other question or comment came from him but she was still aware of him standing there watching her. Her fingers suddenly became all thumbs. 'Haven't you got something else to do?' she snapped irritably.

Silence was the only answer—it was obvious that she had been talking to the air and that he had gone, rejoicing at her pain, to his bed.

With her bandaging completed, she used her left leg for support as she hauled herself up and round from the bathroom stool. She found he was still there.

In her surprise, her right leg suddenly buckled and ready to grab hold of anything to save herself from falling, she clutched at Ryden Kilbane who just happened to be the most available object. Though, for another surprise, it was she who pulled away from him, and not he who pushed her away.

With the thought that she was going to look a right Charlie if he intended to stand there and watch her progress back to her room, aggression rose in her, and belligerently, she snapped, 'Would you mind getting out of my way?'

He moved to one side. She took only one tentative, halting step. 'This is bloody stupid,' she heard him mutter. The next she knew, was that she was not to have a witness to her lurching, staggered efforts to get back to her room, for as though she weighed nothing, Ryden had hoisted her aloft. Whether he felt tainted to have to touch her, or whether he didn't, he was carrying her back to her bed.

Held close to him, Willow made every effort to keep her head away from his chest. Which was how, when he halted in his swift stride, and bent to place her on her bed, his cheek came into contact with hers. The touch of his skin intimately against hers made them both, simultaneously, jerk back. It was obvious that he had construed the incident as deliberate on her part. Willow had suffered enough acid from his tongue to last her a lifetime, and was quick to deflect the insult she felt to be on its way.

'You can cut that out, Kilbane, for a start,' she rounded on him accusingly. For her sins, he dropped her like a hot brick.

Involuntarily, a small scream of pain escaped as her right leg made sudden contact with the mattress. She saw the fury in Ryden's eyes at being accused of attempting a little light dalliance change to that of a man who was extremely fed up.

'Oh God,' he sighed and departed. It was enough to let her know that he found the entire situation as intolerable as she.

Willow had not expected to see him again that night, but, she had just managed to get herself under the covers when he returned with a warm drink and a couple of biscuits.

Her first impulse was to tell him exactly where he could take the cup, saucer, and biscuits, and—more precisely—himself. But he had obviously striven hard to get on top of his sour feelings, and had unbent sufficiently to think that she might sleep better with something warm inside, and so Willow rose over the impulse, and said nothing whatsoever.

'Sorry it's tea,' he unbent even further to apologise, as he handed her the cup. 'The store cupboard doesn't boast a tin of chocolate.'

At that, the hard exterior Willow was trying to build, folded. Swiftly she recalled how she always came to regret it when she softened towards him in any degree. She amended the appreciative thanks, and instead adopted a fairly good imitation of his acid tone, to sarcastically tell him, 'Provided the store cupboard doesn't boast a tin of strychnine either, tea will be fine.'

Willow was never more shattered when, expecting a reply in kind, suddenly, as though her acerbic reply had triggered his sense of humour, the solemn countenance of one Ryden Kilbane, broke up!

And what was worse, to see him grin suddenly, when all for the most part she had ever seen him do was to glower, triggered a response in her, and Willow too, found it funny. A giggle she could not suppress left her.

She still had a smile on her lips that had once been described as wickedly tempting, when she became aware that Ryden's grin had gone. And her smile froze when she saw that his eyes were fixed, as if by some magnet, to the curve of her mouth. Then, before she could draw breath, he had flicked a glance to her green eyes, then, abruptly, he was gone.

Willow did not sleep well that night. During her spells of wakefulness her thoughts returned to that surprising discovery that Ryden Kilbane had a sense of humour. She also remembered the way he had appeared unable to tear his eyes away from her mouth. She could just about credit him with the possession of a sense of humour, but the latter incident, she decided, must be put down to her over-active imagination.

Ryden Kilbane was uncommunicative the next morning. Willow guessed he was bitterly regretting that he had allowed her to make him smile. With nothing more than the odd uncivil grunt coming from him, he brought her a breakfast tray of coffee and scrambled eggs on toast, then took himself off to his office.

She felt wretched with a long drawn out day stretching endlessly in front of her, but she then discovered an unexpected plus, in that her knee was marginally better. Not that she was able to break any records in her hobble to the bathroom, but she did find the marathon trip was much less painful than it had been the day before.

Excitement stirred as she sat on the bathroom stool and completed her ablutions. Perhaps she could ring for a taxi to take her to the railway station? Surely she could get a taxi to Stanton Verney at the other end.

Excitement was flattened though when, on the return hobble to her bed, she attempted to stand up straight—and fell over. More fed up than ever to have to admit that she just wasn't able to go anywhere yet, Willow dragged herself the rest of the way to her bed, and swallowed a couple of pain killers.

But the idea of somehow getting back to Stanton Verney and back to her own four walls, would not die. And when, ever a man with surprises, Ryden Kilbane returned to the flat at lunch time, albeit that he was grim faced and distant, she was ready to stick her neck out and earn some more of his displeasure.

She was heartened when, along with the coffee and sandwiches he placed on the bedside table, he also placed a batch of the latest magazines. He must have a streak of kindness in him, she thought, or why else would he go out of his way to purchase magazines to take her mind off being bored and bed-bound.

'You wouldn't . . .' she quickly found her voice to halt him when it looked as though he thought he had done all he should for her comfort, and looked ready to depart. At the door Ryden halted, but she found not the smallest encouragement in his dour expression when, his impatience apparent, he waited for her to spit the rest of it out. 'I want to go home,' she told him bluntly. One of these days, Willow thought, seeing the sceptical look that came to his face, she was going to take great delight in bashing his head in. 'I'm asking you to drive me,' she added, waspishly, even if she did know that that was no way to ask for a favour.

'I've got something better to do than shuttle you around,' was his snarled rejection of her request.

Willow glared impotently at the empty doorway, the sound of the outer door being closed making her want to start throwing things. If only she had the power to terminate a conversation with him by just walking away. But that was the trouble—she couldn't walk one single solitary upright step without falling over.

If Ryden had been in no mood to have converse with her at lunch time, then when he came home from his office that night, Willow had no mind to talk to him. Not that her disgruntled silence affected him in any way, for no sooner had he fed her, than he went out.

I hope his evening's entertainment turns sour, she thought. Then found her curiosity stirred to wondering where he was and, who he was with. Some elegant sophisticated type of woman would probably suit his taste, she mused. Then she wondered if she was going quietly insane when she found herself reflecting that though, when clad in her Sunday best, she too could look elegant, the sophisticated look might take that bit of extra effort to achieve.

Good grief, she thought appalled, I don't want to be the type of female he admires! Quickly she switched her thoughts on to something else, only to recall how Noel had told her that he and his brother usually only stayed at the London flat from Monday to Friday. That thought made her wonder—did Ryden normally motor down to Broadhurst Hall on a Friday night? If so, was it only because of her, that this Friday, he had stayed in town?

Depression started to set in when she began to have guilt feelings that, because of her, Ryden's parents, who must have been looking forward to seeing their elder son, had been deprived of his visit. His father had been ill, she recalled, and although she had no idea how long Ryden had been in the States, if Mr Kilbane senior was housebound as dear Mrs Gemmill had been housebound, then he would have been looking forward to tonight when his son would come home.

Willow tried to lift herself out of her low feeling by telling herself that if Ryden had agreed to drive her to her home, then with Comberford only seven miles away from Stanton Verney, he would have had no need to cancel his usual weekend at Broadhurst Hall. But, other memories crowded in, and only succeeded in plunging her further into depression.

By the time she heard Ryden's key in the door, her spirits were at a very low ebb. She had tried to find some of her usual optimism by reminding herself that she had a lovely little cottage in a delightful little village, which common sense told her she would soon get back to. But in having thought of Ryden's father, she had also thought of Mrs Gemmill, who up until recently, had been a very big part of her life. She had loved Mrs Gemmill, and she missed her. But Mrs Gemmill was dead.

'Need anything?' enquired a curt voice just as Willow was thinking how she needed the ever cheerful Mrs Gemmill to be with her now.

Tears came to her eyes but, afraid to speak, afraid to look at him lest she gave away her sad feelings, Willow stared at the bed covers, and shook her head.

'Is—everything—all right?' Ryden asked, as if in spite of himself.

Dumbly, Willow nodded, and wished, when she heard him come further into the room, that he would go away. She had a dreadful feeling she might burst into tears at any moment.

She had still not found the stiffening she was searching so desperately for, when Ryden came to a stop at the side of her bed. It did not one single solitary thing to help the effort she was making to pull herself together when, with a sympathy she had given up looking for, he chose that moment to introduce and undermine her with it, when he said, 'You've been in dreadful pain, I know, but try to be brave a little while longer.'

It was the unexpected sympathy that did it. Willow looked up. She looked up into a face that was not grim. She looked up into grey eyes that were not hard but which held a kindliness in them for her so completely alien to the way he usually looked at her. It was her undoing.

'Oh, Ryden,' she wailed, and she had no power to hold back the stray tear that fell to her cheek.

Desperate, lest more tears should fall, she made a sideways jerk to hide her face. But her movement was too quick, her injured knee unprepared, and as a moan of pain escaped her lips, she felt Ryden's arm come about her shoulders. 'Don't cry,' he said gently, his arm there purely as a support for her to lean on as she eased herself into a less painful position.

'I won't,' she promised, and to prove her word, she turned her face intending to smile to show that tears were miles away.

Only her smile never got started. His face was much nearer than she had anticipated. Suddenly, as she recognised that Ryden was neither smiling nor scowling and that his arm about her had tightened its grip—Ryden, his mouth so close to her own, kissed her.

Caught in a weak moment, there was no thought in Willow of mutiny. In fact, as Ryden's kiss deepened, and his other arm came about her, there was no thought in her head, at all.

She had been kissed before, but it had never been like this. As passion flared, she discovered that she liked these new sensations which Ryden was creating in her.

His lips were still over hers when, gently, he pushed her back against the pillows. Willow had long since forgotten her injury when with his hands entangled in her long blonde hair, he eased himself to lie on the bed beside her. Briefly, he broke his kiss, but soon an onslaught of kisses were being rained down on her, and Willow, who had never before been stirred to wanting a man, discovered something else—how easy it was to give into temptation. She felt more vitally alive than ever before. She kissed him in return, invited and was ready to plead for more when he looked to the welcome her mouth held.

She did not need to plead for more. As though the sight of her slightly parted lips was driving him to distraction, fiercely Ryden claimed her mouth.

Through the lightweight bed covers she felt his body against hers. And when one hand left the tangle of her hair to slide her nightdress from one shoulder, she rejoiced in the fire of desire that lit his eyes.

She felt no sense of wonder when, as his lips planted tormenting kisses on her shoulder and the swell of her breast, she realised that he wanted her. It seemed only right, for she—wanted him.

But, that wanting, that seeking to know each other, was abruptly ended. Ryden felt a need to be still closer to her body, and he moved to lie over her. The pressure of his legs caused her to be painfully aware of her injury and a cry broke from her. As though shot—Ryden sprang from her.

'My knee,' she said huskily, and was not sure then which she hated more, the ache that had manifested itself in her limb, or the fact that her cry had taken Ryden from her.

With the passion of her need for him still urgent she looked to where he stood and into his grey eyes, and was shaken rigid to see that there was no answering flame of passion, only the cold hard look to which she was more accustomed.

Her bewilderment was complete when, to match that cold hard look, his voice arctic and holding none of the gentleness she had previously heard, Ryden snarled insultingly, 'Don't congratulate yourself too soon, Miss Cavendish.'

'Con—gratulate?' she faltered, her eyes wide, too confused by what had happened to be able to comprehend what he was talking about. She didn't understand that, in being reminded of her injury, Ryden had also been reminded of his belief that she now had her sights set on the better heeled Kilbane brother.

'Such innocence!' he scorned. 'It never entered your scheming head for a minute, of course, that I might be lulled by sad unhappy tears into forgetting what I know of you.' Her jaw dropped with dismay that he thought she had the ability to cry at will, 'Well, mark this,' he exploded, and seemed then to be as furious with himself as he was with her, 'You may have got me to desire you—for a fleeting moment. But that still leaves it a bloody long way away from any altar.'

CHAPTER FOUR

WHEN Willow awakened on Saturday morning, her thoughts were no less rebellious than they had been the night before. She did not thank Ryden Kilbane that his contemptuous parting shot had put paid to any feeling of being brimful of tears. He had made her too angry for tears. Who did he think he was? It had been *he*, who had kissed her to start with, and not the other way around.

She hated him with all she had that he could, in no time, stir her to such a state of mindless emotion. That *he* should be the one to seduce her womanhood to a point where she had lost sight of everything in her yearning for fulfilment, infuriated her. It had been especially annoying that at the moment when she was lost to everything but the need he had aroused in her, he had turned on her accusing her of deliberately inciting him to desire, for her own devious ends!

Her fury with him and with herself that she had been so weak as to be so incautious when she had been in his arms, drove Willow to desire some kind of action. She could hear Ryden moving around, but didn't care where he was as she left her bed and tested for any improvement in her knee.

Her progress to the bathroom was less painful that morning. And though she was sure there was a definite improvement, she was also very much aware that she was going nowhere in a hurry that day.

Sorely longing to take a bath, Willow resigned herself to the fact that any attempt she made to climb into the tub was going to come to grief. Instead she had a good wash down but it was not the same.

She saw neither hide nor hair of Ryden as she made her snail's-pace journey back to her room, and she was of the opinion that if he was keeping out of her way on purpose, then that was fine by her.

Automatically she headed for bed, then the spirit of rebellion rose within her. Dr Oliphant had said two days' bed rest—well, she'd had two days' bed rest. Enough in her opinion, was enough.

She had rummaged through her case and had found her housecoat and was sitting on a bedroom chair, reflecting that once she'd had a small rest, she was going to get dressed, when the door opened and Ryden, in slacks and a short sleeved shirt, came in.

His eyes moved swiftly from the bed and to where she sat. Willow looked away from him, memories of the way they had been with each other last night darting in to make her tongue tied. But if he too was remembering how they had kissed, then in that initial moment of their eyes meeting, she could not detect it.

She had herself more composed when next she glanced his way but he was placing her breakfast tray down, and was not looking at her. His stern expression though, told her that he had not had any second thoughts about his opinion that she had deliberately set out to ensnare him.

Her anger rekindled when she recalled how clinging she had been to the brute. And when she remembered how he had gone from her room without giving her chance to say even one word, she thought it about time he learned that she was far from clinging this morning.

'I've just about had my fill of you,' she told him tartly.

'The same applies here,' he replied shortly. 'Do you want your breakfast over there?'

'Stuff breakfast,' she spat at him rudely. 'I want to go home. And,' she said, before he could come out with whatever he looked ready to say, 'I can't see, since you've just stated you've had your fill of me too, what good reason you have not to give me a lift.' She was warming to her theme, and would have gone on, but in three short words, he had cut the legs of her argument from under her.

'Neither can I,' he stated.

'You—mean—you'll . . .'

'With pleasure,' he said, leaving her in no doubt that he could not wait to be rid of her. 'Eat your breakfast,' he ordered. 'Then get some clothes on.' He was at the door when a thought apparently struck him, and he turned, his face showing he was sick and tired of the whole wearisome business. His whole demeanour was hostile, when, clearly reluctant, he asked, 'You can get dressed without help, I hope?'

'With both arms broken,' she retorted none too sweetly.

Talk about orphan Annie, Willow thought later, when no amount of tugging at the hem of her skirt would hide the bandage that came well below her knee. She debated about taking the binding off altogether but decided that since they must hit the occasional bump in the road—even supposing Ryden had any thoughts on trying to avoid them—then her knee would be able to survive any jarring that ensued much better if it was strapped up. She had not had to debate on whether or not to wear the court shoes she had brought to team with the skirt. She had to admit however that she looked a proper duck with a patterned skirt and the flat 'sight-seeing' shoes that were meant to go with her trousers.

'Ready?' Ryden briefly enquired when, having given her ample time to get changed, he opened her door.

Willow had not meant to apologise for her appearance, but though his glance at her was only a cursory one, some kind of pride, she supposed, made her tell him, 'I couldn't get my trousers over my leg.'

'Your knee's still swollen?' he enquired as he crossed the room to pick up her case.

'It's gone down a lot,' she made light of it.

Her reply had been noted, she gathered, when without comment Ryden disappeared with her case. Some minutes later he was back. She had been wondering meanwhile what she was going to feel like by the time she had staggered out to the lift, and from there hobbled to his car. She discovered, however, that Ryden had already decided she was not up to making the trip under her own steam.

She did her best to make it appear as though she felt not so much as the tiniest ache as she used her arm muscles to pull herself up out of her chair. No sooner had she got herself vertical, though, than one strong, well remembered arm moved around her shoulders, while his other arm came carefully to the back of her legs, then matter of factly, she was hoisted up.

She guessed she was in for a rough ride, when she experienced several pained moments on that trip to the car park. Ryden halted at a car that looked sleek, powerful, and which must have cost the earth, and told her to lean her weight against it while he opened the passenger door. Willow, on observing that the car was already unlocked, saw that he must have thought it all out in advance. No doubt, since he had not carried her and her case at the same time, he had brought her case down first, and had unlocked his car whilst he was about it.

She then forgot all about his forward planning, because she had to grit her teeth and endeavour to find the most painless way of bending her shape and somehow get her right leg over the door sill.

Once inside the car, she closed her eyes. If any of the

pain she had experienced was reflected in them, then she did not care for Ryden to see it. Moments later her eyes flew wide open when she felt, and then saw, that he was busy propping a couple of pillows beneath her injured limb. Willow was amazed that he should be so thoughtful, when so far as she could remember, they had barely exchanged a civil word that morning!

All thoughts of his kindness were dismissed however, when, as she stared through the windscreen, one car separated itself in her vision from all the others in the car park.

'My car!' she said, pointing to the only car in the area that did not look as though it had a millionaire for an owner. 'What am I going to do about . . .?' Her voice faded when she noted the look of impatience on Ryden's face.

'Hand over your car keys,' he ordered. And to let her know that he never wanted her to darken his doorstep again should she take it into her head to pay a call when she came to collect her vehicle, 'I'll get someone to deliver it.'

Fury filled Willow's soul once again. Even if she wasn't that wretched woman, Gypsy, his own intuition should have told him by now that Willow did not have an avaricious bone in her body, Willow rummaged in her bag for her car keys. Silently, she passed them over.

She knew full well that Ryden was champing at the bit to be off, the sooner to have her unwanted person out of his passenger seat so she was a trifle non-plussed when he did not immediately turn the ignititon key.

'Is something wrong?' she enquired, and turned her head to see that he still didn't appear to be delirious with joy.

'Since I appear to have mislaid my crystal ball—perhaps you'll tell me in which direction you live,' was his sarcastic reminder that she had not told him her address.

Immediately, Willow's head bashing fantasies reappeared with a vengeance, but she resisted, just, the urge to give him something to be going on with. It appeared, she realised, that whatever else he had learned about Gypsy, he had not learned that she lived in Crawley.

'My home,' she told him stiffly, 'is in Stanton Verney.'

She turned to stare through the windscreen, but she knew when he did not immediately set the car in motion, that while he could well be thinking it did not matter very much where she lived, it had obviously not pleased him that she resided where she did.

'Stanton Verney is near . . .' Willow began, just in case he went around with his eyes closed.

'I know where it's near,' he rapped sounding exceedingly put out. 'It's far too near to Comberford for comfort.'

'We all have our crosses to bear,' she told him sweetly, not realising until the car was in motion, that Ryden had not been thinking of himself, but of his brother. With Stanton Verney being so near to Comberford, Ryden apparently thought it would be easy for Noel to bring more hurt upon himself if he could not handle some over-riding need to see the woman who had treated him so heartlessly, but who was still the woman Noel loved.

She guessed that her syrupy, unthinking remark had only endorsed Ryden's opinion of her heartlessness but, since it would not be too long before she said goodbye to her unwilling host, she had no mind to explain, or to try again to put him right about her identity. Her knee was already feeling the effects of the journey and, remembering how furious he had grown with her the last time she had mentioned Noel's name, she had no wish to invite more of Ryden's wrath or perhaps to be pushed bodily from the car and told to walk the rest of the way.

With Stanton Verney coming nearer all the time, Willow grew to mind less and less that all that was coming from her irascible companion, was a stony silence. Soon she would be within her own four walls. She could not wait to be away from Ryden Kilbane, and to slam the door of her cottage shut on him—and his brother Noel too, for that matter.

She was in the middle of the pleasant reflection that the sooner she was home then the sooner she could start forgetting both Kilbanes and what a nightmare her holiday had turned out to be, when abruptly, Ryden broke into her thoughts. He had been morosely silent for so long that the sound of his voice was quite unexpected. Indeed so surprised was she, that in answer to his curt, 'Will your flatmate be home?' her reply came quite without thought.

'I don't have a flatmate.'

The sudden application of his foot to the brakes, and the agony that shot through her right leg, took from Willow any sweet pleasure that he would soon find out that she didn't have a flat either.

'That hurt!' she accused, in agony, and not concerned to spare him her wrath. As she turned her head to glare at him, however, his expression appeared far from apologetic, but more hostile than ever. 'Now what have I said?' she challenged disagreeably.

'I thought—I'm sure Noel said you shared with someone.'

Sadness smote Willow as her thoughts winged to Mrs Gemmill, the person she had lived with. Those thoughts made her voice quiet as she hid her saddened feelings and told him, 'I did share with a friend, until recently. But, I live on my own now.'

'You're lying,' Ryden accused before she could even blink.

'No I'm not!' Willow yelled, on the instant up in arms, not caring at all to be called a liar by anyone.

For two seconds they sat with an angry electric current sparking between two pairs of eyes. His expression told her that he would by far prefer to believe her a liar, than to think he had got it wrong. Ryden looked away from her and began drumming his fingers impatiently on the steering wheel.

That at this late stage, it had occurred to him to query something Noel had told him, however small that something might be, made annoyance spurt in her again. To Willow's way of thinking, it was just too bad. She hid her annoyance though and even managed to smile at the man whose venomous look had turned to one of exasperation, when with saccharine sweetness, she drawled, 'I know the countryside around here is beautiful but really if you don't mind, I should much prefer to get home.'

'And just how the hell do you think you're going to manage with no flatmate there to help you?' he suddenly turned the whole force of his exasperation upon her. 'You can barely crawl, let alone walk.'

'I'll manage,' she told him stiffly.

'Oh, sure you will,' he snarled, at his aggressive best. 'Aside from anything else, you couldn't stand for longer than a minute at any stove, even supposing you'd got any fresh supplies in.'

'I've said I can manage, and I will,' she reiterated, and only then did the hard fact of memory hit home. Her store cupboard was only just one up from Old Mother Hubbard's.

Her green eyes grew wide in panic. By the look of it that weak strain of kindness she had glimpsed appeared to be taking hold in Ryden, and might at least prevent him from just dumping her at the first chance. Her fear mounted. She just could not, and would not, allow him to take her back to that hate filled London flat.

Ryden took his gaze away from her wide green eyes and, clearly having made up his mind what to do with her, set the car in gear and continued in the direction in which they had been travelling. Willow even scoffed at herself that, in her panic, she should have ever thought for a single second that some kindness in his nature would have him turning the car around. She *must* be going potty, she decided, to have thought he would take his feeling of responsibility for her accident that far, that having got her out of his flat he should take her back there because there was no one else to help her. Besides—he wasn't that compassionate.

They had not been driving for long though, when Ryden again stopped the car—with more consideration for her injury this time. Willow's imagination went wild.

There had been a perfectly good telephone back at the flat, she remembered, when, without saying a word, he left the car and crossed over to enter a telephone kiosk. Who was he telephoning? And why? Had he just remembered he had promised to call someone? Or did his telephone call, as she was growing to suspect, have something to do with her?

Trying hard to believe that it had nothing to do with her, Willow watched him when with his long stride he walked back to the car. It was on the tip of her tongue to ask him about his call when he settled himself behind the wheel, but the antagonistic look he tossed her when he caught her eyes on him made the question die on her lips. He'd just love her prying wouldn't he, if he had merely been ringing some girlfriend to confirm a date for tonight?

He started the car, and Willow looked away from him and out through the side window. He was free enough with his sarcastic vitriol, without her inviting more.

Silence reigned again until they were on the final approach to the village of Stanton Verney and Ryden suddenly took a wrong turn. Willow woke up to realise that she should have begun giving him directions to her cottage a minute or two ago.

'We should have turned left back there,' she broke the silence to inform him. 'But, no matter, you can double back at the . . .'

'We're not going to Stanton Verney,' he interrupted her grittily.

'We're n . . .!' Willow broke off as a sign post directing them to the village of Comberford caught her eye. 'We're going to Broadhurst Hall?' she asked chokily, as she tried to get her wits together.

'Clever girl,' he sneered.

Willow ignored the gibe. 'You mean you have to pick up something from your home before you drop me off?' she questioned urgently, Comberford could be around the next bend for all she knew.

'For God's sake, spare me,' Ryden retorted, disgust apparent in every nuance. 'You know damn well you're going to be spending the weekend at Broadhurst.'

'I'm not!' she yelled, agitation hers at his pronouncement. 'I'm not going there. You can't . . .'

'Funny,' he cut her off humourlessly, 'I'd have thought you'd jump at the idea.'

'Well I'm not jumping,' Willow snapped, furious with him, his sarcasm and everything else. 'Stop this car immediately,' she ordered.

Ryden promptly slowed down the car and pulled over on to the grass verge. She soon saw however, that his action was not on account of her ordering him about but purely because it seemed there were a few things of his own he had to say before they reached Broadhurst.

Willow felt a hopeless sense of frustration that with a gammy leg she just could not follow her instinct and get out of the car and hoof it back to Stanton Verney. 'I refuse to go to your home with you.' Determined not to move an inch from the firm stance she had taken, Willow stared unblinking into the hard grey eyes that stared straight back.

'You, Miss Cavendish,' it was then his turn to bluntly state, 'have, since you aren't going anywhere unless I take you there, two choices.'

'I don't need a choice, I know what I . . .'

'Either you come with me to Broadhurst,' Ryden cut in as if he had not heard her interruption, 'or I take you back to London. The choice,' he told her, 'is yours.'

'But I don't have to do either. I have a perfectly adequate home of my own.'

She was just not getting through to him, Willow thought a moment later. For again, just as if she had not spoken, Ryden was itemising the pros and cons, of the two choices he had just given her.

'At Broadhurst our housekeeper, Mrs Stow, will be there to attend to your needs, so too, will my parents. And since I can well do without sex rearing its ugly head, as it did last night,' he bluntly continued, a reminder she could well have done without, 'then I consider Broadhurst the better option this weekend.'

Willow sensed the unsavoury smell of defeat but found sarcasm enough to jeer, 'You're surely not suggesting—should we go back to the flat—that you might forget what a bitch I am and desire me again?'

'I'll grant you're beautiful—though you know that and use it to your advantage—but it was not my sexual appetite I was referring to, but yours,' he rapped back with his usual bluntness. 'You met me all the way when, lulled by sham tears, I allowed physical chemistry to rule—for a brief while,' he tossed in shortly. He continued, without hesitation, to serve her his bluntest statement yet. 'Had I taken you, as you intended, then daylight would have seen me loathing not only you—but myself also.'

It was not very nice to have his hate of her verbally confirmed. Irrationally, Willow, in spite of the fact that she undoubtedly hated him, felt hurt that Ryden had not hesitated in letting his contempt be known.

A feeling of defeat hit her full square as she grappled with that senseless hurt. As Ryden had said, she was just not going anywhere unless he took her there. Suddenly, with her knee starting to cause her great discomfort, she became as weary as him, of the whole troublesome business as he so obviously was. Even so, she had too much pride to give in meekly, and she was able to find sufficient spirit to rally a response.

'To have both me, *and* yourself hating you seems to me to be no more than you deserve. Besides which, I wouldn't give you a second chance to get to me. But,' she went on to have a snipe, 'don't you think, since your home is your brother's home too, that you're taking a bit of a risk?' His thunderous brow told her it was *she* who was taking a risk by mentioning his brother at all but again, her spirit would not let her meekly submit. 'After all,' she challenged, aware she was goading him but unable to stop, 'what's to prevent my telling him I've changed my mind and would like to marry him. Not,' she charged on, determined not to be cowed by Ryden who looked ready to throttle her, 'that I'd want you for a brother-in-law.'

A dart of panic speared through her nonetheless when his eyes glittered so dangerously that she anticipated the feel of his hands on her throat at any moment. With some difficulty, he appeared to gain control of his fury, though his words were little short of savage when he hurled at her, 'We both know what kind of relationship you'd like to claim with me.' As more control came, he underlined for her what she already knew by continuing, 'Don't think for an instant that, were it not for Noel being safe in France, I'd take you within a mile of Broadhurst.'

'If you put it like that,' she answered, with an attempt at false sweetness. She wondered at the devil that had been in her a moment ago, which had made her want to goad him. 'It would appear that Broadhurst is where I shall lay my head this night.'

'As if there was any doubt,' Ryden muttered, to stir her pugilistic tendencies.

Though before she could think up a brilliant retort that might cut him down to size, and seemingly before they were going anywhere he had a word of warning to offer.

'I've learned enough about you to be fully aware that you know which side your bread is buttered. You also know my father has been ill. So, I'll tell you now, Willow Cavendish,' he said heavily, 'that if you *do* anything, or *say* anything, that upsets either of my parents in the *smallest* way, then, I swear it, I'll make certain you'll regret it for the rest of your life.'

That Ryden was in deadly earnest and meant every threatening word, had Willow without any reply. She would liked to have asked what did he think she was that he had to threaten her against upsetting a couple of elderly people but, she rather thought she knew.

Temporarily defeated and lost for words Willow sat, speechless. Ryden accepted from her silence that she had agreed to behave herself and started up the car. Nevertheless Willow's dismay did not stop her from wishing with all her soul that she could be around if the day ever came when he found out the real truth about her. My God, what wouldn't she give to be around then!

CHAPTER FIVE

THE grounds of Broadhurst Hall were impressive and that was before Willow saw the house. The car turned in between the stone pillared entrance. Acres of lawns, trees and rhododendron bushes were spread out on either side of the drive. The house, as they approached, was a two storeyd building with a white stuccoed façade, and with many of the downstairs rooms boasting bay windows.

Even so, as Ryden halted the car, as lovely as the house appeared, Willow would by far have preferred that he had driven her to her cottage. But, since there was nothing she could do about it, when he opened the driver's door and got out, she opened the door on her side.

To extract herself from the vehicle proved as painful as the climb in had been. But Ryden was right there with her and although pride made her want to shake off his hands when he bent to assist her, the sudden jarring pain felt in her knee had her gripping on to him.

'You look washed out,' he said mildly when, again matter of factly, he had caught her up in his arms.

'Thanks,' she replied drily, and oddly, she thought she saw a hint of a grin on his mouth before he turned his head away.

'A room has been prepared for you,' he thought to tell her as he carried her up the steps and through a stout oak door into a wide hall. While it sank in that the telephone call he had made *en route*, must have been to tell his family he was on his way, and with a female visitor, he added, still mildly, 'After I've said "hello" to my parents, I'll take you up—you're probably due for a couple of pain killers.'

'Too kind,' she murmured, but the acid she had meant, was just not there. It must be this peaceful house having a bad effect on me, she thought whimsically. There was no time for more thought, for a slim white haired woman of about sixty, and a tall slim man who looked ten or so years older, and who wore a similar white thatch, had appeared from nowhere.

'Ryden!' beamed the woman who Willow guessed was his mother, and came forward with the man following on more slowly. Smiles were the order of the day then, as Ryden placed his cargo down on a carved oak chair in the hall.

There was much love among the Kilbane family, Willow witnessed, as Ryden introduced her to his parents. The love between Veronica and Clifton Kilbane was plain to see, in the way Mrs Kilbane, after telling Ryden that it seemed he had been in America for a year instead of the month it had been, stepped back and serenely waited while her husband, his speech slow, probably as a result of the stroke he had suffered, had a few words with his son. That love between husband and wife, was something Willow could not recall ever having seen between her own parents. There was love from father to son, from son to father too, she saw. It was all there, when Ryden embraced his father as he had embraced his mother.

'We're forgetting our guest,' smiled Veronica Kilbane when the initial greetings were over. 'Forgive us, Willow,' she apologised, 'but we haven't seen Ryden in an age. Your poor leg,' she went on sympathetically, as her eyes caught sight of the bandage that peeped out from beneath Willow's skirt. 'I'm so glad Ryden could persuade you to come with him,' she added sincerely.

Willow smiled, already warming to this woman who

had somehow produced such a monster of a son. She added 'actor' to the list of names she had reserved for him when, while she still had a smile on her face, she saw him find a smile for her, as he turned again to his parents.

'Willow's about done in. I'll take her upstairs to rest, then I'll join you.'

His smile had faded before they reached the top of the staircase. 'I should be trying to walk on my own,' Willow told him when he took her along a lengthy landing, her own smile long gone. He ignored her hint and did not set her down until they were inside a high ceilinged room, which was fragranced by a vase of lovely full bloomed roses set on a wide window sill.

'Mrs Stow will be here in a moment to help you into bed,' said Ryden, as he placed her in the centre of the mattress.

Willow had had enough of bed. She had dressed with some difficulty that morning and she had no intention whatsoever of undressing and changing back into her night wear until it was midnight at least.

'Are you telling me that, having condescended to bring me into your home, you intend that I shall stay in this room the whole time?' she put the question resentfully.

'It didn't take you long to forget how to smile, did it?' he countered, once more his irascible self. Then, as though realising that their private battles might spill over to give his parents a disturbing hint of his antagonism towards her, he pronounced more evenly, 'That knee needs rest. For that reason, bearing in mind I spotted you trying not to wince a time or two on the way here, you'll stay where you are for a few hours. I'll instruct Mrs Stow to bring lunch to your room. If you're up to it later, you can have dinner downstairs.'

She declined to answer, and Ryden, with no

inclination to wait for her to reply, left her. He had not been gone ten seconds when indignation at being dumped and left to get on with it had her getting off the bed and going to inspect the adjoining bathroom.

She was on her way back and half way to a chair when the plump motherly figure of the housekeeper came in with her case. 'I'll find you a walking stick,' was her practical greeting as she placed the case down and offered her arm. 'I'm Mrs Stow, by the way. Are you going to get into bed or lie on top of it?'

'On top, I think,' said Willow, common sense at last arriving to tell her she would be better off if she had her leg horizontal.

'Come on then,' chirruped Mrs Stow, who put her instantly in mind of Mrs Gemmill, she was so cheerful, 'we'll have your shoes off. I met Ryden at the top of the stairs with your case, I'll go and make you a cup of coffee, then I'll unpack for you.'

Mrs Stow nipped out and came back with the promised cup of coffee, and it was during the next half an hour, that Willow learned not only had the housekeeper been with the Kilbanes for 'donkey's years', but also that she had nursed Ryden and his brother as babies. She learned too, that there were no nicer employers to be found anywhere than Mr and Mrs Kilbane.

Mrs Stow also confirmed the love which Willow had seen among the Kilbanes when she told her how pleased Ryden's parents had been when he had rung to say he had finished his business in America sooner than expected, and that he was now back in England.

'Even when he later rang to say he wouldn't be coming home on Friday after all, but would definitely be here today,' the chatty housekeeper went on, 'it couldn't take away their pleasure that they weren't going to have to wait another week to see him.'

When Mrs Stow finally departed the depression that had arrived unannounced the previous evening, returned once again to Willow. It was on account of her that Ryden had telephoned his parents to say he would not be coming to Broadhurst on Friday. It upset her to think that when Mr and Mrs Kilbane had looked forward to seeing their son last night they had, through her, been disappointed.

Ryden knew they had been disappointed too, and had not been of a mind to let them down again. Which was why, when he had discovered his passenger had no flatmate to fetch and carry for her, he had felt there was nothing for it but to bring a female he could not stand the sight of, into his home.

Willow dwelt for some minutes on that sense of responsibility in him. She recognised that strong sense of duty, that said, because he had been the ultimate cause of her accident, he could not give way to what he would most like to do—drop her off at her home anyway, and go on his way regardless of how she coped thereafter.

She was still feeling low, when Mrs Stow bustled in with her lunch. But as the housekeeper unhooked the walking stick that dangled from her arm, and commented cheerily, 'There'll be no stopping you now, Miss Cavendish,' so Willow's depression began to lift.

'Please call me Willow,' she invited.

By the time she had eaten her lunch, she was consumed with an urgent need to try out the walking stick. Twenty minutes later, she had tried several circuits of her room, and, having got the hang of it, she returned to her bed to rest feeling quite excited that if she went on this way, she would soon be fairly mobile.

Her spirits had come a long way from depression when something made her look at the door, to see that someone was silently turning the doorknob.

'I thought you might be asleep,' laughed Veronica Kilbane, on popping her head in and seeing her house guest was wide awake. She came further into the room. 'Have you got everything you need?' she asked.

'Yes, thank you,' Willow answered. 'Especially since Mrs Stow brought me this walking stick. I've just been trying it out.'

Unlike her elder son, Ryden's mother turned out to be charming. She asked if Willow would like a little company for a while, and when Willow said that indeed she would, Mrs Kilbane drew a chair up to the bed. From then on she chatted away as happily and as freely as Mrs Stow had done, with the only subject not to come up—whatever curiosity Mrs Kilbane might feel—being that of Ryden's relationship to their guest.

Willow had just heard how Mr Kilbane had been forbidden to drive for a while and was thinking how as one with each other Ryden's parents seemed when Mrs Kilbane glanced to her watch, and exclaimed how quickly the time had flown.

'I've delayed you, I'm sorry,' Willow apologised. 'Mr Kilbane will have missed you.'

'I doubt it,' smiled her hostess. 'Clifton likes to hear all that goes on in Ryden's business world—he won't like it at all when I go in and break things up.'

Willow smiled too, she could not help it. Despite Clifton Kilbane's illness and his slow progress back to health, there seemed to be an underlying feeling of happiness in the house—not that she had noticed it very much when Ryden was anywhere near.

'But you'll break things up anyway?' she suggested.

'Ryden won't overtire his father, I know that. But,' Mrs Kilbane confessed, 'while I have to be careful that Clifton doesn't see me as a fusspot, the fright of him being taken ill so suddenly, still has me a bit of a fidget about him.'

Willow well knew the fear and mental fidgeting caused when someone you loved had been severely ill. And although the love she'd had for Mrs Gemmill was not the same as the love which Mr and Mrs Kilbane had shared throughout their years of married life, she could feel every sympathy. There was, though, every likelihood, with Mr Kilbane having had a different illness from Mrs Gemmill, that he would grow stronger and stronger each day, and would live to a ripe old age in this happy home.

When Veronica Kilbane left her, Willow's thoughts were on how it had become apparent that though the two Kilbane sons were much loved by their mother, it was equally apparent that Clifton Kilbane would always come first with his wife.

How wonderful it would be to find a mutual love like that, she mused, and was all dreamy eyed until the memory arrived of her parents, and their unhappy marriage. Of the two, Willow knew which kind of a marriage she wanted, but since there was no one in view on her horizon, she decided she was going to be very careful when the time came for her to select a mate and fall in love.

At that juncture, Mrs Stow arrived with a tray of tea, but this time she stayed only to tell her that they dined earlier these days, since Mr Kilbane was still convalescing, and retired early.

Willow had changed into a fresh blouse, but was still wearing the only skirt she had with her, when just before seven, Ryden came to take her down to dinner.

'I'm sorry I've nothing smarter to wear with me,' she felt compelled to apologise, regretting on seeing him immaculate in a lightweight lounge suit, that she had not packed any of her dressier clothes for sightseeing in London.

'What you have on seems all right to me,' he

answered carelessly. He gave her the very clear impression that she was so beneath his notice, that it hadn't even registered with him how she was dressed. Which, when she did not want him to notice her anyway, still made her obstreperous when he stepped forward as though about to lift her up in his arms.

'I *can* walk,' she announced coldly, and she stretched her hand out for the walking stick.

Before she could get a hand to it though, Ryden had moved to put the stick out of her reach. Angrily, she shot him a withering glance. Then had the shock of her life when, with humour definitely colouring his voice, he murmured, 'A precautionary measure. You sound cross enough to lay about me with it.'

'The idea,' she opined, 'is not without appeal.' Strangely then, all aggression went from her but what was even stranger, was the effort she had to make not to permit a light laugh of shared humour to escape.

'The soup will be cold if we don't get a move on,' he said, to spare her from self-analysis. 'You can practice your walking abilities when there's more time.' And so saying, again as if she weighed nothing, he hoisted her up.

To her confusion as he carried her from her room and along the landing, she experienced the most peculiar sensation at his nearness—at his touch!

She could feel his body, feel his warmth, with every step as he went down the stairs with her. And though she had barely moved a muscle, when he carried her into the dining room, she felt every bit as though she had sprinted a mile. Her heart raced and she felt all choked up inside—— so much so that it was not until he had placed her on a chair at the table, and had taken his arms from around her, that she realised that although the pain in her knee had been part and parcel of her ever since the accident she had not been conscious of feeling pain at all!

There was no time then to dwell on that lack of pain, or on the peculiar emotion that had taken its place. For both Mr and Mrs Kilbane were greeting her. Willow got herself sufficiently together to be able to reply pleasantly, then found that this happy house was playing the oddest of tricks on her.

As she looked down at her plate she observed that the starter was not soup, but paté and it dawned on her that Ryden had used the ruse that the soup would get cold to silence all argument that she could walk. She flicked a glance to him and saw a quick of movement at the corners of his mouth. Once again, she felt the most absurd urge to laugh.

She did not laugh, however, but turned her attention from him and to his parents. She was used to conversing with people her senior so one word soon led to another and the meal progressed smoothly. She could converse quite naturally with Ryden's parents and because Mr Kilbane's speech was slow she waited with warm unfussy sympathy for him to form his sentences. Meanwhile she was overwhelmingly conscious of the many times Ryden—no trace of humour in him now—would glance her way.

She knew then that he was alert to every word she said, and should she utter one syllable out of place, he would quickly turn the subject and be all set to sort her out later.

It was more obvious than ever that Ryden was taking in her every word when Mrs Kilbane made some reference to her son Noel and his marketing abilities, and said how she was sure he would do a splendid job in France.

Willow's memory of Noel was that he was easy to talk with—a must, she thought, for anyone in marketing. His personality was such too, she recalled, that she had been completely without anxiety when he, a slightly inebriated stranger, had been in her sitting room.

'I'm certain he will,' she agreed, her thoughts still with her memory of Noel. Instantly she became aware of the dark look which Ryden was sending her.

'Do you know Noel?' Veronica Kilbane asked.

Oh crumbs, Willow thought. She was sure that to claim to know Noel was not going to upset anyone but she was able to see from the steely glint in Ryden's hard, grey eyes, that he was not well pleased that she had invited his mother's question.

She delayed in answering but Mrs Kilbane who, on observing how her glance had gone to Ryden, made a simple deduction, and answered her own question.

'Silly of me,' she said lightly. 'It goes without saying that with my two sons so close, that you've met Noel. Do you live in London?' she asked.

On safer ground, she hoped, Willow revealed that she lived in Stanton Verney, whereupon, Clifton Kilbane offered the slow comment that Stanton Verney was only down the road. As he stretched his memory, he recalled how only this week, he had read in the local *Courier*, that there was apparently a great hullabaloo going on in her village about some car-driving lout who'd churned up the village green.

Willow was glad that she had been able to prevent his younger son from being named as that 'lout'. 'The village green preservation group are very committed,' she murmured.

Thankfully, the subject was lost when Mrs Kilbane remarked how Ryden had said that she lived alone and then enquired after her parents.

'My parents are divorced, and married to other people,' Willow answered. And although relieved to be on safer territory, she felt she ought to explain—even though everyone, save Ryden, had made her feel that they wanted her at Broadhurst—why he had not been able to take her to her one of her parents' homes. 'My mother and her husband live in Hong Kong,' she said, and added, as an afterthought, 'I seldom see my father.'

'Oh, my dear,' Veronica Kilbane sympathised, 'You're virtually all alone in the world!'

Willow had never seen it quite like that, nor had she looked for sympathy. Before she could find some bright and breezy answer however, her hostess was warmly saying, 'Ryden told us you could only stay for the weekend, but I insist you stay with us for much longer.'

'We'll see how Willow's injury improves,' cut in Ryden before she could decline. But she knew, before he pleasantly took the conversation into other channels, that he thought she had purposely angled for the invitation to extend her stay, and that he was as mad as hell with her on account of it.

That made her mad too. She had not done any angling! It wasn't her fault that the conversation had drifted the way it had! She hadn't seen the invitation coming, or she would have tried to deflect it. It wasn't her fault, that he had a warm and generous hearted mother!

Willow had said little more by the time the meal came to a close. She was still inwardly fuming that Ryden was not prepared to believe that the most innocent of comments she made did not have some nefarious design behind it.

Her hate for him spiralled even higher when his father rose to his feet and stated he would spend some time in the drawing room before he turned in.

Ryden, as if not prepared to give her another opportunity to angle for anything else, promptly declared, 'I'm sure you'll excuse Willow if she doesn't join us. The car journey down was quite a strain.' He smiled at her, though she noted there was no smile in his eyes, when he tacked on, 'And although Willow won't admit it, she's still feeling the effects and is in need of her pain killers.'

Unable to obey the urge to thump him, and powerless to take to her heels, Willow was forced to sit there and, in reply to Veronica Kilbane's concerned question, answer that it barely hurt at all.

No sooner had Mr and Mrs Kilbane gone from the room, than Willow was resolved on one issue. Ryden Kilbane had made her feel like a leper, and it was for sure that he did not want her presence contaminating the drawing room. Well, since he felt that way, even if she had to make it to her room on all fours, she'd be damned if she would let him lay so much as one single uncontaminated finger on her to assist her.

'Don't touch me!' she said when he took a step in her direction. 'Don't you dare touch me!' she spat at him, seething with indignation. 'I can make it on my own.'

'Don't be so . . .'

'If you lay a finger on me, I'll scream,' she told him, her voice starting to rise. She hated him the more when after just one more step nearer, he halted.

Painfully, she struggled up from her chair, her fury with him not abated that it was not her that he cared about, but that any scream that came from the dining room might alarm his parents.

How she wished then as she made her hobbled way through the door that she had thought to bring that walking stick with her. Stubbornly determined to make it on her own, she did not care how much it hurt.

The hall she had lurched across was wide, and had little in the way of furniture for her to hang on to, so by the time she had reached the bottom of the stairs, she felt as sorely in need of her pain killers as Ryden had suggested she was.

'Oh God,' she groaned, as she hung on to the newel

post. The stairs seemed to be as high as Everest. Even when the pain in her limb started to defeat her rage, Willow was still stubbornly determined that she was going to make those stairs unaided.

That was until the matter of choice was taken from her. Suddenly, unheard by her, so hard was she concentrating, Ryden was right there with her.

'You've got more guts than brains,' he commented tersely, his swift all seeing glance taking in her ashen face, and the moisture on her brow.

'I want nothing from you,' Willow seethed, as his arms came out.

'Pull the other one,' he scorned grimly, and whether she wanted any help from him or not, in the next second she was up in his arms, and he was carrying her up the staircase.

At his touch all her anger suddenly evaporated, and the confusion she had felt before, was with her once more. Although she was no longer exerting herself, her heart was racing wildly. If there were words that should be said, words such as, 'Put me down immediately' she could not think of them nor, as that chokey sensation returned, was she capable of saying a single syllable.

She had still not surfaced from the mêlée of emotions that were cavorting inside her when Ryden strode with her along the landing. The only sound to come from her was when he opened her bedroom door, and in taking her through the opening, hit her right foot against the door frame.

Her small mew of pain was barely audible. Gently Ryden eased her on to her bed and she guessed the small sound had teased through his anger to remind him how her leg could be jarred by any careless contact.

Ryden still had an arm at her back when Willow looked up, and straight into his eyes. She suddenly felt breathless, and more confused than ever, for whatever else she did not know, what she was aware of was that she did not want him to take that arm away. Indeed—she wanted both his arms about her!

Without knowing it, she had a hand on his arm and when she saw that there was no hard glint in his eyes, but that some warmer light had taken its place, Willow gripped tightly on to that arm. For long seconds they stared at each other, and it seemed the most natural thing in the world that their lips should meet.

Her heart raced as if fit to burst to feel Ryden's mouth against her own. Eager to have him kiss her, and kiss her again, and to never stop, she clung to him.

But, suddenly, abruptly and painfully, the kissing stopped. And the familiar sound of Ryden's loathing of her rent the air. He cared not, then, what pain any jarred movement inflicted. Furiously he tore her clinging arms from his shoulders. And he turned on her furiously.

'Damn you!' he reviled her. 'Damn you, and your physical charms.'

If her sleep had been fractured the previous night because of the pain in her limb, the pain that kept Willow awake that night, was from a very different cause. There was a giant-sized ache in her heart that no amount of bandaging would cure. It had been there ever since Ryden had so furiously damned her and her physical charms and had not delayed to leave her room.

That he should revile her so when he had enjoyed those kisses as much as she, should have made her instantly furious too but Willow was not furious. She had no need either to analyse why it was she had not yelled something pertinent to his departing back. For the startling truth of just why his touch could make her heart race, had broken. Utterly stunned, all anger had been nullified.

She had not wanted to believe that truth but, to her dismay, Willow discovered that no matter how much she argued, 'How can it be?' or, 'It can't be!' and 'It's crazy—I don't even like him!' there were some truths that would not go away.

However hard she tried to tell herself, throughout that dreadful restless night, that her imagination had always been lively at the best of times, the truth of what had happened was still there. No amount of trying to put it down to her imagination, would alter that truth.

Only that day, she recalled, she had decided that when it came her turn to fall in love, she was going to select that person most carefully. But the truth of the matter was, that love had chosen for her. She had fallen in love with Ryden Kilbane, and there was no escaping from that fact, just as there was no escaping from the fact that Ryden Kilbane was entirely the wrong person.

CHAPTER SIX

SUNDAY got underway with more evidence for Willow of the caring household she was in. First Mrs Stow, as ever cheerful, came in with an early morning cup of tea, and asked if she had slept well, and if her knee was any better.

Willow lied about her fitful night's sleep, but replied—so much else was weighing her down that her injury had taken second place—that her knee had much improved.

Then, when Mrs Stow went out, and before the thoughts that had kept Willow awake could bombard her again, Veronica Kilbane, still in her housecoat, came into her room, with more or less the same enquiry.

Forced to lie again about her wretched wakeful hours, Willow found a smile to tell her hostess, 'The swelling has gone down, and my knee feels much easier.'

'Oh, good,' beamed Veronica Kilbane. 'Now you mustn't do too much too soon, but if you feel like getting up after breakfast, Ryden can bring you down and you can put your feet up on the drawing-room sofa.'

Willow smiled again, in agreement, but no sooner was she on her own, than she was out of bed to test her leg. That she was still not going to break any records for long distance walking was obvious but her knee was indeed easier and that was about the only bright spot on the landscape.

She was back in bed by the time Mrs Stow arrived

with her breakfast. 'I'll come back and help you to dress later,' she pleasantly offered, the news that Willow was forsaking her bedroom for the drawing-room obviously having reached her.

'I'm sure I can manage,' Willow thanked her and, with one thought starting to dominate her mind, she waited only until the door had closed, then with more haste than was usual she quickly disposed of her breakfast, and left her bed.

She had no idea, as she washed and dressed, how she was going to feel when she saw Ryden again, or how she was going to act. The nonsense he could make of her when he touched her, had her resolved that, no way was he ever going to carry her anywhere again. Once she judged breakfast was over downstairs, she was going to be ready to make it to the drawing-room under her own steam.

She found it impossible to keep thoughts of Ryden and the love that had sprung up in her for him at bay. Why that love had come, or how love for him could have surfaced when his kindnesses to her had been few and far between, were questions that defeated her.

All she knew, when she thought the time had come for her to try some abseiling down the stairs, was that this new emotion bore the responsibility for other previously unknown moods and emotions that had taken her.

She must, she realised, have started to fall in love with Ryden from almost the first moment of seeing him. She had felt contrary with him on a couple of occasions, when contrariness had never before been in her nature. Her subconscious must have known before she did what was happening—why else had her self-defence mechanism activated itself? Her fury with him when she had not wanted him to carry her to her room last night, had surely been over the top, even if to be made to feel like a pariah, was enough to anger anyone. Her subconscious must have known then, that to be held in his arms was what she really wanted. Her self-defence mechanism had come into play, as if to prevent her from learning what she had, and to guard her from feeling the way she did now.

She had found no joy in the discovery that she was in love with Ryden. What joy could there be, when all he felt for her was hate?

As if to escape her thoughts, Willow went as quickly as she could out on to the landing. She had been certain that everyone would be downstairs but she had progressed no more than a few yards when she heard the sound of a footfall behind her.

Straight away she knew who it was. But as her heart picked up its beat, and warm colour surged to her face, so she made herself keep on in her aimed direction.

'Ambitious?' enquired Ryden mockingly, too soon there at her side.

Love, again, made her contrary. 'You know that already,' she snapped. But as she felt her flush of colour subside, she just could not resist the urge to look at him.

Oh God, she thought, I do *truly* love him. Even as all trace of mockery disappeared and his mouth firmed at her reminder that her ambitions went higher than a mere junior partner, Willow knew that the feeling inside of her could not be put down to any figment of her imagination.

Ryden was still at her side when she limped to the head of the stairs. And suddenly, when she knew he was hating her like hell, Willow could no longer take that hate. She had to tell him the truth. She just had to risk his wrath by speaking his brother's name. She wanted Ryden's love, not his hate.

'Ryden . . .' she said, and broke off. She needed to get

what she had to say phrased correctly, and looked from him as she cogitated on the best way. Then she saw that the moment was not be, because Mrs Kilbane was passing the bottom of the stairs, and had looked up, her face starting to show alarm when it appeared Ryden was not going to carry her down.

'Willow has her independent hat on this morning,' Ryden called down to his mother. 'She was just about to ask to be allowed to try the stairs on her own.'

The moment when Willow would have attempted to explain everything to Ryden was gone, but as she haltingly began to negotiate the stairs, the idea still remained. She knew then, with Ryden taking the stairs with her ready to catch her if she stumbled, that at her very next opportunity, she was going to bring up his brother's name, and take the risk of getting her ears singed.

Exonerating herself was not going to make Ryden fall in love with her, she thought, but at least she would feel better if he knew he had no cause to hate her.

At last, she reached the bottom of the stairs, but she was so taken up with what she intended to do, that even the sting behind Ryden's, 'So now we all know how clever you are,' hardly penetrated.

'Well done!' Mrs Kilbane congratulated her on her unaided achievement. 'But that's enough independence for a while. Put your arm through mine,' she instructed, 'and lean on me, and we'll settle you in the drawing-room.'

'I thought I'd take Willow for a drive,' Ryden stated before Willow could comply and hook herself on to his mother.

Excitement soared in Willow. To be alone with Ryden in his car would give her the very opportunity she wanted to tell him everything.

Veronica Kilbane however, was shaking her head.

She then relegated Ryden to her son, and not the head of Kilbane Electronics, when firmly, she told him, 'Then you must think again Ryden. Willow is too uncomplaining to tell you herself, so I'll tell you for her—her experience yesterday of being driven over bumpy country roads with a bruised and badly sprained knee, is one too painful to be repeated so soon. Even,' she added, 'if your car does happen to have the latest in modern suspension. Besides which,' she smiled to their guest, 'I want Willow to stay and talk to me this morning.'

Willow guessed that it was precisely because he had heard she was to occupy the drawing-room sofa and did not want her to have close contact with his family, that he had offered to take her for a drive in the first place. But the disappointment she felt that another chance to tell him everything had gone, was to fade when she learned that he had not intended she should be his sole passenger anyway.

'In that case,' he told his mother pleasantly, keeping whatever chagrin he felt well hidden, 'it'll have to be just Father and me.'

A couple of hours later, Mrs Stow bustled into the drawing-room with a tray of coffee and, with the cheery comment that the weather had improved to be more like summer, thank goodness, out she bustled again.

Ryden and his father had long since departed for their drive, and Willow's conversation with Mrs Kilbane had ranged from embroidery to the merits of Gilbert and Sullivan, when Mrs Kilbane placed her empty coffee cup down and commented on the peace and quiet and made a reference to how the house always seemed to take on a buzz when Ryden was around. Willow could not hold down the urge to want to know more about him.

'Do you miss Ryden—now that he lives away during the week?' she asked.

'He's had his London flat for some years now, so we've adjusted,' her hostess replied. 'Though it's only since his father's illness that Ryden had made sure that either he or Noel are here at the weekend.' She smiled. Then, as proud as any mother to talk of her sons, she continued, 'It went without saying, of course, that as soon as Noel had finished with university and Ryden made him a partner, he'd offer his spare room to Noel if he wanted it.'

'Ryden . . . the London flat belongs to Ryden?' Willow questioned, only just holding back a gasp. She had been under the impression that the flat was half Noel's! Never would she have taken advantage of that key he had left behind had she not thought that the flat was half his!

'What's Ryden's, is Noel's,' Mrs Kilbane told her happily. 'It's been the same ever since Noel was born—I'm pleased to say.' She then went on to confide with her usual warmth, 'Ryden was eleven when I found myself pregnant for a second time. It gave me many an anxious moment worrying how he would feel, when he'd been an only child for so long, to have a baby brother or sister.'

'You worried needlessly,' Willow stated with her first hand knowledge of how protective of his younger brother Ryden was.

'Completely needlessly,' Veronica Kilbane agreed. 'Noel arrived on Christmas day, and I'll swear Ryden thought he was the best Christmas present he'd ever had. He used to spend all his pocket money on him,' she recalled. And went on to recount how, when Noel had left babyhood he would toddle everywhere after his brother, so that soon, one never saw one without the other.

'Didn't they ever—fight?'

'Oh, they had the occasional brotherly squabble,' Mrs Kilbane confirmed. 'But with Ryden that much older than Noel, it never came to fisticuffs, and the day never ended with them being bad friends.

'Ryden's very protective of Noel, isn't he?' Willow put in.

'I suppose that's natural enough,' her hostess considered. 'It was always Ryden to whom Noel took his troubles—seldom me or his father. So I expect since Ryden had been solving his troubles and putting him on the right road ever since he can remember, it's now instinctive in him to watch out for him. He . . .' Mrs Kilbane broke off as the clock on the mantel chimed midday, and when it had looked as though she could happily talk of her sons for another half an hour or more, instead, she exclaimed, 'Good gracious—is that the time?' And with a slightly guilty look for the time they had spent in conversation, 'It seems an age since I've let myself forget everything to indulge in the pleasure of female company. But,' she said, leaving her chair, 'since Mrs Stow would be put out if I didn't peer over her shoulder occasionally, I'd better go and see how lunch is progressing.'

While Mrs Kilbane had been with Willow, there had been no space in which the despair of her love for Ryden could get to her. No sooner was she alone however, than thoughts on the hopelessness of her love for him, resurfaced.

Sorely then, as heartache began to bite, and unhappiness started to dig deep, did she want her hostess to return. Forced to inactivity, Willow desperately needed action or some subject to talk on which would take her thoughts away from the fact that her love had no future with Ryden.

With no one there to talk to, and her thoughts on

Ryden too defeating to be taken lying down, Willow roused her fighting spirit to decide she would not be forced to accept inactivity. She had done no more than swing her feet to the floor though, when the burden in her heart was ligthened to hear the sound of Mrs Kilbane returning.

Willow looked to the door as she relaxed back against the sofa, but when the door opened, and a fair-haired young man came in, her eyes widened in startled surprise.

She was not the only one to be surprised for, halting where he stood as he caught sight of her and recognised her, Noel Kilbane's mouth dropped open.

'What. . .?' broke from him. Then, a smile curved his surprised mouth as he closed the door, and came over to where she sat. 'Don't tell me I left you the wrong key?' he quipped with comic relish.

'I wish,' replied Willow severely, not sure, as she said it, if she meant it or not, 'that you had never left any key behind.'

At her tone, all humour immediately went from his face. And, as his glance caught her bandaged right leg, he asked swiftly, 'What's been happening?'

A few minutes later, with Noel's only interruption, 'You mean—Ryden's back too?' leaving out only her new found love for his brother, Willow had told Noel most of what had happened.

'Oh, Lord,' he groaned, as it sank in that on Wednesday she had taken him up on his offer to have a holiday at the London flat, only for Ryden to attempt to turf her out when he had mistaken her for Gypsy. 'But—why on earth didn't you tell him you weren't Gypsy?' he asked, looking dumbfounded.

'Don't think I didn't try,' Willow replied. 'I've *told* you—he was furious.'

'Oh, Lord,' he groaned again. 'I've seen Ry when he

gets his dander up—you might just as well hit your head against a brick wall as try to get through to him.' He was obviously appalled that when he had only wanted to return a kindness, she should have received such terrible treatment. 'But, he treated you well—when he knew you'd hurt yourself?' he asked.

'He—accepted responsibility for the accident,' Willow told him. 'And even though I know he didn't want to bring me to Broadhurst, when I let slip on the way to my place yesterday that I didn't have a flatmate, he brought me here.'

'Which means, if I know my brother, that while he might have fed and watered you, you've had very little other comfort.'

Willow closed her mind to those moments when she had felt the warm comfort of Ryden's arms, and tried to concentrate her attention on other comforts. He had brought her some magazines, she remembered. Then, afraid that if she mentioned any of the occasions, few though they had been, when Ryden had not been a total brute, that she might reveal more than she intended, she simply said:

'He thought I was Gypsy.'

'Well, he won't for much longer,' Noel assured her. 'I'll go and tell him straight aw . . .' Abruptly, he stopped, and suddenly such a stricken look came over his features, that Willow promptly forgot she had been about to tell him Ryden was not in, and that he had taken his father out for a drive, to urgently ask:

'What is it? You look as though . . .'

'Oh, God,' groaned Noel, sinking down into the chair his mother had earlier vacated. 'It's only just hit me—if Ryden, because he thinks you're Gypsy, has been as aggressive with you as I know he can be, then what chance is there that—the real Gypsy will be served any better when they meet?'

'They're going to meet!' Willow exclaimed. 'But—I thought you and Gypsy were through!'

'So did I,' Noel agreed. 'I was sure of it, otherwise I would never have whinged on about the expensive gifts she'd accepted, and all the rest of it when Ryden rang me in Paris. God,' he writhed, 'I must have sounded pathetic.' Rising over a moment of inner squirming, he went on to tell her, 'Even after I'd given Ry chapter and verse on the cruel way in which Gypsy had rejected my proposal and told me to sling my hook and had promised I'd heed his advice to chalk her up to experience and forget her, I found that to forget her, just wasn't that easy, so—yesterday, I rang her.'

By the look of it, and after all that had been said, Noel was still keen to pursue Gypsy. Willow saw how very much in love with his ex-girlfriend he was. With a new awareness of love, and just how utterly impossible it was to cancel a love given where it was not wanted, her voice was gently understanding, when she pressed, 'You rang her?'

He nodded, and admitted, 'I was shaking like a school boy while I waited for her to answer the 'phone. I was expecting a very frosty reception but Gypsy couldn't have been sweeter.'

'So,' said Willow, taking it slowly, 'things are back to normal between the two of you.'

'No, not yet, and that's the point. They're never likely to be, if Ryden has anything to do with it,' he said, looking worried. 'Gypsy has agreed to see me tomorrow night but I just can't risk Ry finding out that it's she and not you who is the girl I love, before I find out where I stand with her.'

'But he can't do anything to harm——'

'Oh yes he can,' Noel interrupted quickly. 'Don't you see,' he said, starting to look desperate, 'that I shall never get my relationship with Gypsy back to our old footing once Ryden knows that you're not Gypsy? Once he's laid into her like he laid into you, I'll be lucky if she ever speaks to me again, much less agrees to see me.'

'But, he wouldn't do that—would he?' Willow asked faintly, as it dawned that she wouldn't put it past him.

'I'm so mixed up, I don't know for sure,' Noel confessed. 'But I just can't risk Ryden going to see her. She'd never forgive me that.'

In Willow's view, Noel had started to sound as mixed up as he said he was. If he was not seeing things straight, then it was easy to see that the reason lay in the fact that he was desperately afraid that something might go wrong with this second chance he had with his girlfriend.

'But,' she said, searching for logic, even when she knew from personal experience that where the heart was involved, logic just didn't apply, 'how is Ryden to know that you've taken up with Gypsy again? You don't have to . . .'

'He'll know.' Noel stated, as if he knew it for a fact. 'He'll know on the nights I'm not home 'til late, that I'm seeing some female. Ryden was never slow in putting two and two together, and having put two and two together, the rest will fall into place.'

'But,' Willow still tried, her heart sinking as she saw her hopes of telling Ryden the truth start to slip from her grasp, 'Ryden doesn't even know where Gypsy lives.'

'He knows the sort of work she does. It wouldn't take him long to ring round the agencies until he found the one Gypsy works for. I need time,' he said then. 'Time to slip in a word here and there to try and correct the impression I've given my brother that Gypsy has no heart and only has her eye to the main chance. I know him, Willow,' he stressed. 'I just can't take the risk of him thinking that it's in my long term interest to go and sort her out. Why,' he said, sounding appalled as the most awful thought suddenly struck him, 'he might even mortally offend her by offering to buy her off!'

Perspiration had started to break out on Noel's face. Seeing the state he had got himself into, the agony of mind that was his, Willow ended what had started out so promisingly, but what had gone down and down the more they had talked it out.

'You want me to give you that time?' she asked.

'Would you?' Noel pleaded. 'Would you let things remain the way they are with Ryden still believing that you're Gypsy?'

The words of agreement would not leave her tongue, but the nod of her head was all Noel needed to see. Impulsively he leaned forward and took hold of both her hands.

'It won't be for long,' he promised, a never more grateful smile there in his relief. 'If I can just use you for cover until I know where I am with Gypsy—until Ryden knows that my long term interest lies with Gypsy . . .' He interrupted his flow, to suddenly endorse, 'It's not really deception on your part because you've tried to tell Ry who you really are. And although it's the first time in my life that I've ever deceived him, Gypsy is so important to me that . . .' Again he broke off, though this time, because the door had opened.

Both pairs of eyes shot to the door. Willow inwardly quailed to see Ryden and his father standing there. She recognised a look of total fury in Ryden's eyes as his blistering glance took in what she had forgetten—that Noel still had hold of both her hands!

'Noel!' The glad cry had come from Clifton Kilbane to see his younger son was not in France, but was right here in the drawing-room.

At once Noel let go of her hands and hurried over to greet his father. Willow, meanwhile, having no part to play in these proceedings, tore her eyes away from the hostility that blazed in a pair of fierce grey eyes. And, with her eyes fixed anywhere but on the man she loved, she heard Ryden join in the conversation, his fury pushed out of sight because his father was there.

'I thought your negotiations with Monsieur Ducret were due to start this weekend?' she heard him address Noel.

'They were scheduled to begin tomorrow,' Noel replied. 'But I've had to cancel the meeting on account of Monsieur Ducret contracting some virus or other. I've left word where I can be reached as soon as he's up to any in-depth business talk. So, since it's only a quick flip over the Channel, and I can be with him within a few hours of his call, I thought I'd come on home.' Noel's voice had lightened when he added, 'Had I known how Gypsy—Willow had taken a purler, and that you'd brought her here, I'd have come home sooner.'

If Ryden had any reply to make to that, Willow did not hear it. For Veronica Kilbane had come into the room, and as she exclaimed her surprise on seeing Noel, and then embraced him, Clifton Kilbane came over to where she sat.

'Did you have a good drive?' Willow asked, as soon as he had made himself comfortable opposite her.

'It was good to be outside,' he answered. Soon they were into a discussion on the various shades of green which nature produced at this time of year in trees and hedgerows but at no time was she unaware of Ryden talking with his mother and Noel over by the door. She was aware too that his conversation was not so earnest that he could not spare time to let his eyes glance every now and again, to where she sat talking with his father.

When lunch was announced, it was Noel who was the one to come over to help her to her feet.

'I can manage fine now,' she told him, when on her feet, and she took a firm hold on her walking stick, and moved a step away.

Lunch proved to be a happy family affair, with Ryden, in spite of whatever dark thoughts were going through his head, saying not the smallest uncivil word to her. She was not, however, deceived by his pleasant outward manner. Willow knew full well that it was out of consideration for his mother, and more particularly on account of nothing being allowed to upset his father, that the few comments that did come her way were without their usual vitriol tip.

That Ryden could not consign himself not to have a go at someone, became plain as lunch ended. To Willow's relief though, it seemed that it was to be Noel, and not herself, who was going to be the one to bear the brunt of his wrath, for, when a general move was made to leave the table, Ryden turned to his brother.

'If you've nothing planned for this afternoon, there are a few things I'd like to go over with you in the study.'

'Give work a rest, Ryden,' his father slowly chipped in. While he and Ryden passed a few comments, Veronica Kilbane suggested that Willow might like to again occupy the drawing-room sofa.

'Would you mind very much if I went up to my room?' Willow asked, needing to be alone to consider the situation now that she had agreed to let Ryden continue in his belief that she was the girl Noel loved.

'Of course not,' smiled her hostess. 'Have a nice rest this afternoon then perhaps you'll feel like staying down with us after dinner tonight.'

Willow then became conscious that Ryden's conversation with his father had ended, and that everyone was tuned into what she and Veronica Kilbane was saying. As Mrs Kilbane turned to make some remark to her husband and they both walked towards the door, it was Noel who offered his assistance.

'I'll just give Willow a hand to her room, then I'll join you in the study, Ry.'

'I want,' said Willow quickly, able to detect a grimness in Ryden even if she was not looking at him, 'to try the stairs on my own.'

'But you can barely walk!' Noel protested. Only to have Ryden seal the matter, when he cut in,

'Willow is feeling independent today. Let her sense some small feeling of achievement—for a while.'

All Willow sensed, was that there was a barb in that remark somewhere. She was not waiting to hear any other gem that might drop from his lips so she gathered her concentration for the mammoth task she had set herself.

Her progress up the stairs, was painful and slow. It was not until she had laboured to the top and had paused to lean against the landing rail, that she glanced down to see that both Noel and Ryden had been standing in the hall, and had watched as she went.

'Three cheers for independence,' she tossed down to them, and saw Noel smile, and Ryden favour her with a grim look that seemed to include a reiteration that he thought she had more guts than brains.

Her bed, when she finally collapsed on to it, was bliss. Willow was soon to recover from her exertions though, and, as she had known would happen, Ryden was again there to dominate her thoughts.

She remembered how he had not minced words to tell her that were it not for Noel being safe in France, he would not take her within a mile of his home. She recalled how furious Ryden had been when he'd returned with his father and found Noel, not in France, but holding hands with her in the drawing-room and it suddenly occurred to her, that Ryden could be saving a few more unminced words to hurl her way!

Oh heavens, she thought, her mind lighting on what Noel had asked her to do—she had no defence! For by giving Noel, by a nod of her head, her promise, there was no way now could she explain anything to Ryden.

When she considered the matter though—since pigs would fly before ever Ryden fell in love with her—what had she lost? Nothing, came back the answer, except a cast iron defence when next Ryden had a go at her—and a chance to have him apologise that he had got her all wrong.

Which, she decided on thinking about it, could, if he put two and two together as sharply as Noel had suggested he was able, might cause Ryden to suspect that any revelations she made about herself, stemmed only from the fact that she wanted his apology—that she wanted him to notice her in her own right—that she felt something for him!

At that point, Willow decided that Noel was not the only one with mixed up thinking. Her love for Ryden, she saw, was diminishing her powers of logic. Any thought that he might receive so much as a glimmer of a suggestion that she felt something other than hate for him, was sufficient for her to know that she would stay quieter than a church mouse on the subject of her identity.

Willow closed her eyes and wondered what was going on in the study. She guessed Noel would have the utmost difficulty to lie to his brother. Which meant that Noel must be turning himself inside out to not lie to him, but also at one and the same time to make sure he did not pick up so much as a whisper of the truth.

Mrs Stow standing by her bed with a cup of tea, roused Willow to the realisation that she had dozed off into a light sleep. 'I thought you could do with this,' the housekeeper said cheerily. 'I've brought you a couple of biscuits too since Mr Kilbane has said that, after a lunch like we had today, he doesn't want to see another crumb until eight.'

'We're dining at eight tonight?'

Mrs Stow said they were and, her look more cheerful than ever, she went out commenting happily, 'We're getting back to old times.'

Willow sipped her tea, but she was still too replete from a full-treatment Sunday lunch, to manage another morsel. But with hours to go before eight, she was suddenly visited by a restlessness to be doing something. Even so she had no wish to go downstairs when, depending on what had taken place between Ryden and Noel in the study, she could be called upon to field remarks which, if misfielded, might lead to all sorts of complications. And life, she thought dully, as she left her bed and limped to the bathroom, was, at the moment, quite complicated enough.

Having made it to the bathroom with the intention of sluicing her face Willow's glance took in the pink of the bath. On thinking of the hours she had to kill before she presented herself downstairs and egged on by her success in ascending the stairs unaided, she was fired to scale another mountain. It seemed years since she had last taken a bath.

Not too long afterwards, she was lying with water up to her chin. Deprived of a bath for days now, when to bathe daily was her habit, the warm, fragrant luxury was sublime. Even the nagging ache in her knee appeared to have gone.

Willow savoured every moment of a delicious wallow and, defeated in her attempts to keep Ryden out of her head, she let her thoughts roam to how she had expected him to say something about taking her to her home tonight, but how he had not. It was only a short trip to Stanton Verney, she mused, he could well have planned to drive her there after dinner. Or maybe, she went on to consider, either he or Noel would drop her off at Stanton Verney on their way to London in the morning. Though, would Ryden. . .? Abruptly, her thoughts ceased.

Suddenly, she picked up a sound that told her someone had come into her bedroom. Mrs Stow, she thought. Mrs Stow had come to collect her tea tray.

But it was not Mrs Stow. Agitation had already started to set in when, only then realising that she had left the bathroom door ajar, Willow heard a firm tread come nearer and nearer.

Hurriedly, that tread known to her, she sat up and twisted her head round to stare in horrified fascination at the doorway. All she knew then, as she sat frozen rigid and unable to put those advancing footsteps down to her imagination, was that Ryden, no doubt still furious that she and Noel were under the same roof, had come to look for her and that, since Ryden could not find her in her bedroom—he must be too furious to want to leave until he had found her!

CHAPTER SEVEN

WILLOW still wanted to believe that Ryden held a few qualms about coming into the bathroom to seek her out but then the bathroom door was suddenly pushed even wider, and she was made to believe that he held no such qualms. She was galvanised into action but on the instant of making an attempt to shoot out of the bath and get a towel around her, a reminder that she had an injury was swiftly, and painfully, brought home.

Yet even as pain screamed through her and forced her to splash down again, so at her first glimpse of Ryden, she gave vent to her frustration and temper.

'Get out!' she shrieked. 'Get out of here!'

She was angry, frustrated, and not a little covered in confusion. She also hated Ryden with every fibre of her being. He was not taking a blind bit of notice of her shrieked commands. Prepared to look anywhere but at him, she presented him with her profile, only to meet the tough look of him in the mirror panelling in front of her.

Warm colour surged through every part of her—if she could see Ryden reflected in that mirror, then he in turn was able to have full view of her. It was, though, to her back that he addressed a scornful:

'You're surely not suggesting my brother is the only one to see your naked form.' And to confirm that there was nothing wrong with his eyesight, 'Not a bad form at that,' he added mockingly.

'Will you leave!' Willow yelled, near to tears and unable to take much more. 'You've obviously got something to say that won't wait,' she said hotly, when her shouted request was ignored, 'I'll join you next door in . . .'

Relief entered her being when Ryden started to move. Intending to cover herself with all speed, her hands went to the sides of the bath in another attempt to lever herself out. Only, it was not that simple.

She swallowed down a cry of pain as she slumped back into the water. But, alarm and agitation were swift companions again for, when she braced herself to make another stab at it, she had done no more than gripped hold of the porcelain when suddenly, firm hands seized her upper arms. And before she knew what was happening, she had been plucked bodily from the water.

Struck dumb to find the bath mat beneath her feet, no sound left her as she stood naked before Ryden. She was still too dumbfounded to say a word while his glance raked down her and, as if drawn by some magnet, his grey eyes returned to fasten on a small droplet of water that seemed determined to linger on her left breast.

Her stunned eyes full on him, she saw a muscle jerk in his temple—it was that small movement that snapped her out of her speechless trance. Though before she could reach the towel she had made a grab for, Ryden was there before her. In the next moment, the towel had been thrust at her, and he had gone to wait in the other room.

To discover that she was shaking, was no surprise. But as agitation started to hop about inside her Willow, fearing that Ryden might come back into the bathroom, wasted no time on trying to compose herself. On tenterhooks lest he returned, she decided she had no time to dress, and she took down a fresh towelling robe that had been hooked on to the back of the door. As she did so, however, she could not but wonder at that muscle that had jerked in Ryden's temple.

She felt flattened when she reasoned that such an uncontrolled spasm at his temple had not meant he had been moved in any way by her nakedness. She could take it as read that she was not the first woman he had seen unclad so it was more likely that to see her thus, had stirred in him nothing but a resurgence of loathing.

A sound from the other room was all that was needed to remind her that she had better make haste. Dispirited, and still damp, she tied the towelling robe securely about her. She then took up her walking stick and limped to join him.

Ryden's hate had knocked the stuffing out of her but the sour look he tossed her way when he saw her, deflated her beaten spirit even more.

She was conscious of his brooding hatred the whole time she limped across the floor. Suddenly, as she came to a halt by the window, Willow knew that she was going to fight tooth and nail to hide what, just to see him, could do to her and her emotions.

She wasted no time about it either when, her voice as uncaring as she could make it, she took the battle into his camp and drawled in his general direction, 'I imagine your diatribe begins, "Leave my brother alone".'

'That goes without saying,' Ryden rapped back toughly, the narrowing of his eyes telling her he was not enamoured with her tone. 'You've hurt him enough,' he snarled, 'without making him suffer further at your grasping talons.'

Willow stood firm at Ryden's downright distrust, but she knew before they went any further that the role which Noel had asked her to play, was going to leave her ragged.

'Noel and I had a—a disagreement,' she said, and got as far as, 'All lovers fall out occ . . .' when the glint that came to Ryden's eyes, unsteadied her. 'We all say things in temper which we don't really mean,' she made herself plough on.

'And often reveal in temper that which we've been at pains to keep well hidden,' he trounced her.

'That too,' she had to agree, privately of the opinion that the latter was probably true in Gypsy's case. But—she had given her word to Noel—she would have to try to carry off the part, a struggle though it was. 'But Noel knows . . .'

'Noel's so damned crazy about you, he doesn't know anything any more,' Ryden sliced in fiercely. 'Within five minutes of seeing you again, you had him believing that not only had you overreacted in temper when you told him when it came to marriage that you preferred someone of my standing, but also—being a past mistress at dangling the carrot—you left him wide open to more hurt, by giving him hope to believe there might be a chance that you love him!'

There were a couple of conversations which Willow would not have minded being full privy to. The one between Gypsy and Noel for one, and it would have been a help to know some of what had been said between Ryden and his brother in the study. But, in the absence of knowledge to everything that had been said, she was left to play it by ear, and to try not to give Noel away at the first hurdle.

'How do you know that . . .' she broke off when the spirit that was part of her character nudged her to respond, '. . . since I've learned to my cost what a disagreeable swine you are—that I haven't come to my senses, to realise that I do care for Noel?'

Willow knew at once she had said the wrong thing. 'That's a lie!' blasted her ear drums. Ryden looked murderous. 'There's only one thing you care for,' he thundered, 'and that's to latch on to any man, whether he's a swine or not, so long as he has the wherewithal to feather your nest.'

That hurt! Even if she knew deep down that Ryden thought he was addressing his brother's avaricious girlfriend, it hurt. Reeling from his onslaught, even when Ryden came menacingly forward so as to make her wonder if she was going to get out of there alive, she just could not turn tail.

Aggression was pushed to the surface by that hurt, and the essential spirit in her refused to be beaten. Offensively, she jibed, 'It would be more hardboard than feathers, if I waited for you to come across.'

Immediately Willow knew, from the stilled look of him, that Ryden had misinterpreted what she had said. A moment later, he revealed a new sort of toughness and let her know what it was he thought she had meant. 'Are you suggesting,' he asked curtly, his eyes hard like granite, 'that should I make it worth your while financially—you'll leave Noel alone?'

Willow felt crushed that he had misread her so—the hurt was indescribable. That Noel had been afraid Ryden might say something of the sort to Gypsy, and that Gypsy might be mortally offended, was of little consequence to Willow then. Because it was not Gypsy who was on the receiving end, but her. Bleeding inside that Ryden still did not know her better than that, Willow had suddenly had more than enough of the Kilbrane brothers.

'The only thing I'm suggesting,' she surfaced to flare, 'is that you take yourself *and* your offer, and leave me alone. And that goes for your brother too,' she added, spurred on the more his insult took root. 'In fact,' she declared hotly, 'it would suit me well, if I never saw the pair of you ever again.' And to endorse that statement, 'I shall *not*,' she said with emphasis, 'be downstairs for dinner this evening.'

'If I believed that, I'd believe anything,' Ryden sneered. 'You might have my brother taking every word you utter as gospel, but I know how your devious mind works.'

Willow had no clue to what he had read into what she had just said this time, but she was past caring, and had not the smallest inclination to find out.

'Believe what you like,' she tossed at him, 'I'm still not coming down to dinner.'

'You're sure as hell not having dinner in your room,' Ryden told her curtly, when her thoughts had been more that she would sooner go without than sit at the same table with him. 'I'm not having Noel making time with you under this roof, when he comes to find out why you aren't joining us.'

'That thought was never in my mind!' she gasped.

'Of course it wasn't. Never for a moment did it cross your greedy little brain to consider the cosy time that could ensue with you and Noel in this room together.'

'That's a . . .' Willow started to fly. She broke off as it hit her that she was on the sticky end of this argument. With double quick speed she changed tack, and in the next second, her voice treacly sweet, she was purring, 'What a spoil sport you are, Ryden. How can you deny Noel when, at your flat, were it not for my injured knee, you were all for a "cosy time" yourself?'

'You were willing,' Ryden slammed at her harshly.

Willow did not care to be reminded just how willing she had been; for all she had been the one to start this. 'It must be your fascinating charm,' she retaliated, her falsely sweet tone gone.

'It's for sure it didn't take me long to have you begging for more,' he did not hesitate to further remind her.

The knowledge of her love had shown her exactly why it had not taken him long to have her clinging, but, on the defensive suddenly, and not liking it, her voice was surly, when she told him, 'I—wasn't myself then.'

'You're more yourself now?' he scorned, to let her know that was something else he had no belief in.

Willow hardly knew what she was any more, even if in facing that she loved him, it did explain for her this new contrary person she had become—this person who had emerged to act outside her normal way of behaving. Even her normal way of thinking had been turned upside down.

She had not liked his last scornful remark though, and she felt it incumbent upon her to let him know, that in starting to recover from her accident, that she *was* more herself, and that never again would she ever be so weak as to cling to him the way she had done that time.

'I *know* I'm different,' she told him haughtily, when pride demanded that she show him a lofty attitude. 'At your flat . . .'

The rest never got said. The words she had ready, died on her lips when she saw him start to move that short distance nearer. Carelessly he threw her stick from her and his hands closed round her arms. As she looked up into his eyes, Willow read that Ryden had just lost patience with trying to exact some verbal truth from her.

Her throat dried so that not even the smallest word of protest could she utter. As his head came down, Willow knew that, when they had been swopping insults from a distance, her haughty manner had been instrumental in deciding him to prove a truth which could not be gained from her any other way.

His mouth was over hers before she could stop him. But that did not prevent her from pushing at his chest with all her strength; though with her balance poor, her efforts to put some space between them amounted to very little.

'Stop that!' she cried, when he freed her mouth to seek the contours of her throat, determined that, since to kiss her meant nothing to him, he was not going to make her cling to him as she had done before.

'When I'm ready,' he gritted. She gave him an outraged push and succeeded only to lose her balance completely. 'Allow me to take your weight,' he mocked when she toppled against him. He did not wait to have her permission but picked her up in his arms and carried her to the bed.

'Will you . . .' Willow began furiously, when she felt his chest come over hers to pin her down, but only for her 'get off me' to never get uttered.

'With pleasure,' he cut in, and again his mouth claimed hers, while one hand slipped inside her robe to caress her shoulder.

'You swine!' she hissed, fear starting to make itself felt at the dent just the feel of his caressing hand made in her determination.

'Kiss me, beautiful,' he instructed, and raised his head to look into her eyes.

'Never!' spat Willow. But, just as if that word was a challenge to him, Ryden renewed his onslaught on her mouth.

How many minutes ticked by while she concentrated all she had on not giving in, she could not have said. With each kiss, each caress, it became more and more difficult for her to remember just why it was that she must not give in to Ryden.

Soon, she thought, he must stop. Soon, he must admit defeat. But, as he continued to play havoc with her emotions, so he began to stir a need in her.

Oh God, I want him, Willow thought, unable to deny to herself the fire he had kindled and, in admitting to herself that she was on fire for him, so she seemd to lose all wish to resist him.

For when, gently this time, Ryden laid a feather light kiss against her mouth, he did not have to force her lips apart. Voluntarily, her lips parted, in submission and in invitation. She knew not where she was any longer, and had forgotten all except that she wanted his caresses, that she felt starved for him, and that she needed his kiss. When he broke the light touch of his lips against hers, the only fear in Willow, was the fear that he was going to deny her, her need.

But he had said 'Kiss me, beautiful' and she stretched her arms up and around him, and holding him to her, mindlessly, kissed him.

Gently, Ryden returned her kiss. His hand beneath her robe caressed its way to her breast and as it was captured, so the pressure of his mouth over hers increased.

'Oh, Ryden,' she moaned, her body starting to throb with her need when his fingers tormented the hardened pink tip that topped the swollen mound cupped in his palm.

She was in a no man's land of wanting when, her robe untied, the folds eased back, Ryden trailed kisses over her breast, her stomach and her thighs.

She was ready to beg him to take her while one hand caressed her hip and his mouth took possession of her left breast. His other hand teased and tormented her right breast. The hand at her hip and his touch at her breast, intimately caressing, pushed her up on to a more urgent plane of wanting. Her breath came in short gasps and she cried out, 'Oh Ry,' in ecstasy, oblivious that she had cried out the shortened version of his name which she had only ever heard his brother use.

She was soon made aware of her mistake when suddenly, there were no hands to caress her and, shattered, she saw that Ryden had moved with lightning speed from the bed.

Her open mouth showing that she had not yet worked out what had happened, there was the flushed warmth of passion on her face and reflected in her eyes, when she looked to where Ryden stood.

While she could discern that same warmth of colour from their lovemaking on Ryden's face, to her bewilderment, she could see no trace of warmth in his eyes.

It was then that she hit the ground with a thump. There was no passion in those grey eyes; in fact, there was nothing there, but the cold, hard look with which she was more familiar. She could not believe what her eyes were telling her, nor did she want to believe what his icy arctic look was saying.

She was made to believe it though, for, before he left, his look as contemptuous as his words, Ryden took the trouble to tell her:

'You're no different from the female who was mine for the taking back at the flat, sweetheart—you've just proved that. Just as you've proved that Noel's not the only man for you.'

Her love for Ryden would have seen her willingly give all he asked but he cruelly debased what for her had been an act of love, when, he stated bluntly, 'You'd be mine, or any man's—if it was to your advantage.'

Speechless, that he should reduce what for her had been a love filled time to nothing more than a physical level—an opportunistic physical level on her part—Willow watched him go. Then the pain started.

An hour later, she was still hurting, her only salvation being the knowledge that to have so demeaned what had been so earth shaking an experience for her down to the level he had, must mean that her secret that she loved him, was safe from Ryden.

Another hour went by—and Willow started to get angry. She was glad of that anger, it helped to ease the aching void that had been inside her ever since, without a care for her, Ryden had closed the door.

It was that anger that had her going against her inclination to stay in her room. She would be at that dinner table tonight—if it killed her.

Willow was still inwardly fuming when, with ten minutes to go before eight, she left her room. She did not think Ryden would come to escort her down the stairs, but since she did not want him to so much as come near her ever again, she was not going to leave a thing to chance.

She batted away the memory of how near, how close, he had been when they had held each other in their arms, and with each negotiated stair tread, she silently berated him. Despite the contemptuous way he had left her and in spite of the fact that his lovemaking had been based only on his intention to prove she was no different, that swine had desired her, and had wanted her, she knew he had.

A temporary halt was called to the list of names Willow had given Ryden when, as she neared the drawing room, the door opened.

'I was just coming to get you,' said Noel just as Ryden, as she suspected, not far behind him, appeared.

'Beaten you to it,' she replied on a light laugh. And when Mr and Mrs Kilbane started to emerge from the drawing room too, for their sakes she hid her animosity toward their elder son. 'Hello Ryden,' she greeted him pleasantly, 'I'll soon be taking the stairs two at a time at this rate.'

She switched her glance from him to smile at his parents, but she had not missed the way one of Ryden's eyebrows had ascended in surprise that, when if she had taken a swipe at him with her stick it was no more than he deserved, she was acting as if that passionate episode up in her bedroom had never happened.

Throughout dinner that night, Willow kept up every appearance of being a contented guest in a happy household. Included in all conversation, she readily joined in, and spent minutes in chatting to both Mr and Mrs Kilbane and when required, she passed a remark here and there with both Ryden and Noel, but favoured neither one more than the other. By the time the meal was over, no one, not even Ryden—whom she had caught giving her a glance of suspicious puzzlement one time—could have gleaned the mass of seething indignation she was inside.

She was determined that Ryden Kilbane would never know the chewed up mess he had made of her. So when Veronica Kilbane said, 'You're not going straight to your room tonight are you, Willow?' even though she would liked to have done nothing better, conscious that Ryden thought she could not wait to get to her room—and to have Noel follow her—Willow smiled.

'I'd like to stay down for a while, if that's all right.'

'My dear,' said her hostess, and to let her know that nothing would please her more, she came to hook her arm into Willow's. 'It's a delight to have some female company in this male dominated house.' Together, they led the way to the drawing-room.

Though quite when in the next hour or so that followed Willow lost sight of her anger, she did not know. The time that had started out at a crawl when at Mrs Kilbane's insistence, she settled on the sofa, had suddenly flown. Conversation had sometimes been general, and at others Veronica Kilbane had engaged her in some topic while the three men, led by Clifton Kilbane's interest, talked about micro-computers.

At half past ten it suddenly came to Willow how much she was enjoying being part of a super family evening—she knew it was time for her to go to bed. The object of the exercise had not been that she should enjoy herself, for goodness' sake! Her sole aim in coming down those stairs at all, had been purely because pride had demanded that Ryden should not know how he had all but finished her off.

Honour, she thought, grasping to retrieve some threads of indignation, had been satisfied.

'Look at the time!' she gasped, after a glance to her watch, though she knew full well what time it was from the clock on the mantel. 'I think I'd better say good night,' she murmured as she eased her feet from the sofa.

'Do you have to go?' asked Noel, 'It's early yet, and . . .'

'The doctor ordered Willow should have a certain amount of bed rest,' Ryden chipped in to decide the matter.

That he said this in spite of his knowing that she had already complied with the doctor's instruction to have two days' bed rest, showed Willow clearly just how much he wanted her out of the family drawing-room. It was all she needed to have her indignant anger against him return.

'Ryden's right,' she said, and sent a smile his way so he should know that it did not matter a button to her that he would prefer to have her out of their company. 'The sooner I get to bed, the sooner I shall heal, and the sooner shall I be able to resume my usual lifestyle.'

Take that, she thought, and was in the act of saying good night to Mr and Mrs Kilbane, when Noel volunteered to help her to her room.

'Please don't, Noel,' she begged, as she hid a surge of rebellion on catching Ryden's grim look that said he was wholeheartedly against Noel going to her bedroom with her. 'I've done little of any consequence all afternoon,' she said sweetly, quite well aware that

Ryden could hear every word, 'I really should be trying to get more exercise.'

Quite proud of her parting shot, Willow was still congratulating herself when, having lumbered up the stairs with more thought to her knee than elegance, she limped along the landing. Though when, her door but a few steps away, she heard the sound of someone striding along behind her, all feelings of patting herself on the back abruptly departed.

She had known it was Ryden even before, unable to make it into her room, she halted at her door. As she looked up into the face she wanted to hate, but which she knew she did not, so her sorely stretched acting ability gave up the ghost. She wanted to remain the same outwardly pleasant person she had been all that evening but her heart started to hammer and her contrary self-defence mechanism awoke, pushing her in the opposite direction.

'You'll forgive me,' she said, her hand on the knob of her door, her voice short, aggressive, 'if I don't invite you in.'

She did not go much on the smile that came to his features that, without his having said a word, he had aroused her aggression. Nor did she care at all for his silky tone when, intent on mockery, he slowly drawled:

'Whatever happened to sweet Miss Butter-wouldn't-melt, who said good night, a few minutes ago?'

Willow glared at him. Love him she might, but she was of no mind to let him walk all over her or to have a long protracted argument with him either.

'Just in case it hasn't registered, Kilbane,' she snapped, 'while I don't give a damn about you, I do have some regard for your parents. Whether you believe it or not—which is entirely immaterial to me—I'd pretend to like the devil himself, before I'd upset either your mother or your father.'

She had not expected Ryden to be aghast at her laying it on the line so she had no cause to feel disappointed when, although his mockery had gone, he showed no sign of clutching his heart.

'So the Miss Sweetness-and-light bit downstairs was an act for my parents' benefit,' he stated, and seemed then to be more considering than shattered that she felt so little for him. 'Which proves,' he went on, 'that you at least care enough not to give them a moment's stress.'

So it seemed Ryden, whom she did not doubt had been watching her every move ever since he had brought her to Broadhurst, had found something to her credit from his observations. Her heart gave a giddy leap. But—he had dropped her from a great height before.

'I'm tired,' she told him bluntly. 'If you've got something to say, then say it, and let me . . .'

'Your knee is acting up?' he asked sharply.

'It's improving by the hour,' she snapped, not thanking him for his concern at this late hour. 'But that still doesn't mean I'm fit enough to take up jogging again.'

That she was apparently one of the nation's jogging fraternity, was of no interest to him. To her surprise though, he gave her a second credit, by telling her, 'You've shown a tremendous amount of pluck over that knee.' And, while she was trying to steady her heart after it took another giddy leap, Ryden went on, 'But for all you've tried to make light of your injury, you're still not in any condition to live on your own yet.'

From where Willow was standing, she couldn't see that she had any other option. But, having searched round for some short, sharp retort, she got as far as,

'Well, that's my . . .' only to be chopped off, when he added, reluctantly, she thought,

'Which means, that when I return to London in the morning, I'll have to leave you at Broadhurst.'

Incredulous, it took Willow a second or two to comprehend that with Ryden now in possession of proof that she would not do anything to cause his parents' stress, even if he felt the utmost reluctance to leave her in his home, that responsibility which he had accepted for being the cause of her accident, had left him with no other choice.

'My God!' she gasped, mockery winning over tears that would have fallen with the realisation that even with a couple of credits ticked up, his reluctance showed he still had a very low opinion of her. 'Surely you can't be serious?' she choked. 'Surely you're not really meaning to leave me here?' The fierce pain that only he could create in her began to bite and Willow grabbed at all the sarcastic venom she could find. 'With both you and Noel gone, aren't you afraid I might keep my hand in by making a play for your father?'

'There are times,' Ryden grated between his teeth, his hands clenched fists at his sides, 'when I could cheerfully hammer you to a pulp!'

Willow heard the door to his room snap decisively shut, before she had made it half-way inside her own. 'Damn him,' she muttered furiously but tears were stinging her eyes—he had already hammered her to a pulp, without ever laying one physical blow on her.

CHAPTER EIGHT

NEVER, thought Willow when, on a lounger in the garden, she took advantage of the late afternoon sun, had a Monday ticked by so slowly. She had no need, however, to wonder why that Monday in particular should take such a wretchedly long time to drag by—Ryden was not there.

She had tried to get interested in the book in her hands, but she absorbed nothing of its content. Again and again her thoughts would stray to the man to whom she had given her heart. Whether she fight him, be upset by him or even hate him, she still had to admit that life had lost its sparkle without him there at Broadhurst Hall.

Suddenly she felt ashamed, for everyone had been most kind and had gone out of their way to make her feel wanted that day. She had opened her eyes that morning to find a beaming Mrs Stow standing by her bed with a cup of tea, but she had felt a dullness of spirit ever since Mrs Stow had told her, 'That's the two workers off,' and let her know that Ryden and Noel had left for London. 'Now we can concentrate on you,' she had said.

Mrs Stow had found her some fresh strapping for her knee, and although Willow had been in two minds as to whether or not she still needed the strapping support, because Mrs Stow had troubled to find the dressing for her, she had wound it on.

She had then gone downstairs, feeling some apology was due for the fact that she was still there now that Ryden had gone but she had found that Mrs Kilbane would not listen to any apology.

'Nonsense,' she had told her with a smile. 'I particularly asked Ryden to come after you last night, to endorse my invitation that you stay with us a little while longer. I couldn't have been more delighted,' she went on, 'when he came to my room this morning to say that you'd agreed to stay.'

Agreed to stay! Willow's thoughts were again back with Ryden. She was just reflecting, not for the first time that day, how his reluctant 'I'll have to leave you at Broadhurst' had held little invitation to it, when Veronica Kilbane came and joined her in the garden.

'Clifton's in the garage poking about with things greasy under the bonnet of the car,' she informed her as she took her ease in a deck chair next to Willow. 'It alleviates some of his frustration at not being allowed to drive just yet, I think.'

Willow, in need of some activity herself, knew all about the frustration of having one's wings clipped, and she sympathised for a moment or two. Then, as an afterthought, she asked her hostess if she was a car driver.

'Don't get me started on my efforts to become a female Niki Lauda,' Veronica Kilbane said on a hoot of laughter. 'Clifton swears his hair was the same colour as Ryden's until he attempted to teach me to drive. For the sake of his blood pressure,' she grinned, 'I gave up trying.'

A warm friendliness having grown up between them, they were still in the garden at half past six, with no need for either of them to look for a topic of conversation. But whenever an easy silence fell, Willow's mind would stray. Ryden's hair was as black as night, and he wouldn't be home again before Friday. By Friday, she would, somehow or other, have made it back to her own home.

She was anxious to be gone before Ryden came

home, and her thoughts went to consider—since to walk so much as a quarter of a mile would crease her—just how she was going to make it back to Stanton Verney. Willow drew a blank.

She had just gone into the realms of wondering if Mrs Stow could drive, and if Clifton Kilbane would lend his housekeeper his car, when the sound of masculine footsteps on the flag stones set into the lawn, had all thought ceasing.

To look up and to see Ryden making his way over to them, when she had thought never to see him again, was like having a bolt of high voltage current shot through her. Joy, unbounded, unthinking, entered her heart, just to see him.

If Willow was careless of anything save that Ryden was home, she was also oblivious of the suddenly enlightened glance Veronica Kilbane gave her as she returned to Willow the book that had jerked from her lap. If the older woman had any curiosity about what, if anything, her elder son felt for the young woman he had brought home, or what Willow felt for him, then about the latter, her hostess had just seen the answer.

'It's most unusual for Ryden to come home on a Monday night,' Mrs Kilbane said thoughtfully, then suddenly her expression changed to one of twinkling delight, as she teased gently, 'I wonder if the fact that you're here, Willow, has anything to do with it?'

Willow could only blame that having thought of little else but Ryden all that day, to so unexpectedly see him made her forget completely that the last time she had seen Ryden, he had stated a desire to hammer her to a pulp. At Mrs Kilbane's comment, Willow's joy knew no perimeter, and as Ryden came to a stop not a yard from her, she was for a few delirious seconds, swayed to think that it was because she was there, that he had not stayed in London.

A smile started somewhere deep within her as he answered his mother's greeting. That smile of welcome, was still shining in Willow's green eyes when Ryden looked to her. When his glance stayed on her, and strayed to her upward curving mouth, his attention held for what seemed an age, and her heart raced fit to burst.

Before she could get vocal release from a suddenly dry throat, Ryden had abruptly turned from her, to casually ask his mother, 'Where's Noel?'

'Noel?' exclaimed Mrs Kilbane.

'He's not here?'

Veronica Kilbane shook her head. 'Should he be?' she asked.

'He left his office early. I thought . . .'

Whatever Ryden thought, Willow did not want to know. Ice cold water had just doused her fantasies. Suddenly aware of her folly, her smile rapidly disappeared. She must be a crass, deranged idiot, to have thought for as long as even a quarter of a second, that Ryden had broken with his usual practice of not coming home until Friday on account of her. It was on account of his brother that he was home. His sole purpose was to see that Noel did not again become entangled with a female whom Ryden considered the lowest of the low.

'We're not dining until seven-thirty,' Mrs Kilbane was saying, when Willow tuned in again. 'Perhaps Noel will have arrived by then.'

The time had come, Willow saw, to let Ryden know that her beaming smile of welcome, had been put on solely because his mother was there.

'It could be,' she said, at her contrary best as she turned a cool look on him, 'if Noel didn't specifically state he was coming home to Broadhurst,' she offered a serene smile, 'that he left his office early because he has a heavy date elsewhere.'

Dinner, that night, was not a happy meal for Willow. She found it a constant strain to pretend it had not affected her to know that Ryden, even if he did think she was someone else, strongly objected to any possibility of having her for a sister-in-law.

Whether love had made her irrational, or whether it hadn't, to her way of thinking, she had been in Ryden's company sufficient times now for him to have seen for himself that she was just not the type gold-digging harpies were made of.

Somehow she managed to smile and to chat her way through the meal, but, when it was over, Willow knew that there was no way she was going to be able to move to the drawing-room with the others to smile her way through the rest of the evening as she had done last night.

Before she could make it known that she was going to have an early night though, Ryden's mother was saying that she and Clifton were following a serial on television and so as not to bore anyone else with what would be a tedious plot if they came in half-way through, they were going to watch television in the sitting-room.

Oh, my giddy aunt, thought Willow, by then having received enough of Mrs Kilbane's warmth, to know that never would she be so churlish as to exclude her from joining them normally—Mrs Kilbane thinks she is giving Cupid a helping hand! She thinks that Ryden and I want to be left alone together!

Grappling with her embarrassment, Willow smiled, and said she hoped that the serial came up to expectations. Left alone in the dining-room with Ryden, certain that he too had seen through his mother's ploy to give them some time alone, Willow waited only until she heard a door up the hall close, then she, too, was off.

Without a word of good night to him, she made for the dining-room door. Though with her progress still tortoise slow, he was there long before her to pull the door wide. She limped past him and headed, not for the drawing room, but towards the stairs, only to find that he had come after her.

'My brother didn't make it for dinner,' he observed, for all his smooth tone, giving her the impression that he was hell bent to get her to rise to his bait.

'So I saw,' she said quietly, refusing to bite.

'Which means . . .' Ryden drawled, only the slight narrowing of his eyes there to tell her that her quiet answer had annoyed him, 'you could be right.'

'Right?' she queried, totally without heat. That too, appeared to annoy him.

If he found her passive reaction irksome, though she would have thought it a pleasant change from the way she usually fired up at him, then he overcame it, to explain silkily, 'It could be,' he broke off to smile pleasantly, 'that Noel does have a heavy date—elsewhere.'

Willow knew exactly where Noel was, and with whom he had a date. She smiled. 'Then good luck to him,' she said sweetly, her mouth widening to give Ryden the benefit of her perfect, even teeth.

Ryden did not like her broad smile any more than he liked the fact that she was refusing to be needled—Willow saw that from the way his jaw firmed. She sensed however that it was going to be her turn not to like something when, as she made a move to go on her way, by the expedient of placing a hand on her arm, he halted her.

Forced to stop, she looked up into chilly grey eyes. If Ryden had been after some sign of reaction from her, he received it, when he arrogantly told her, 'It would appear—when there was never any likelihood of you getting your hooks into the senior partner . . .' he refused to let go of her when she tried to pull out of his hold, '. . . that you've muffed any chance you had of getting your claws stuck into the junior partner.'

Willow tried desperately hard to stay cool—but failed. 'In that case,' she flared, glad to feel hate surge up in her for Ryden, 'I might just as well go home.'

No sooner had the words left her, then bang went any façade Ryden had of being even tempered. Aggression was there in full force when he furiously flung her arm from him and, as if fearing he might yet commit murder, before he turned and strode away, he snorted, 'You're going *nowhere* until *I* say so.'

Wide awake in her bed that night, with the house quiet and with everyone else asleep, Willow realised that Ryden could not be nearly as sure as he would have her think that she had lost all chance with Noel. Because, with her knee improving daily—and he had witnessed for himself that she was now capable of hobbling about—why, if it wasn't that he wanted to keep his eye on her, and Noel, was he insisting that she did not leave Broadhurst until he said so?

In despair, her hate for Ryden short-lived, Willow knew that, since love had brought her nothing but grief, in the interests of self-preservation, she somehow had to get away from Broadhurst.

The answer to how that might be achieved, came half an hour later when, with everything silent, she heard a car coming up the drive. Noel, she thought. And as he entered the house and came up the stairs, then passed her room, she made her plans.

Aware that both Noel and Ryden would leave for London early, Willow was up and dressed and with her ears tuned at the door for the sound of every footstep the next morning.

She heard Ryden go by, but he was not the one she was listening for. Ten minutes later, a set of footsteps she knew less well, went by. Though by the time she had opened her door and had limped out on to the landing, Noel was half way down the stairs.

'Noel!' she called on an urgent whisper as she went as quickly as she could after him.

Her prayers were answered when he heard her whispered call and retraced his steps to meet her at the top of the stairs.

He guessed, inaccurately, at the reason for her urgent call, and said, by way of apology, 'I did try to get you alone on Sunday night, but Ry wouldn't have it. Not that there was much to tell you about what went on in the study that afternoon,' he went on glumly. 'Ryden didn't want to know about Gypsy's good points, and wouldn't believe she had just been hasty in her temper. I didn't just then want an extended discussion which might have seen me lying my head off so, apart from saying that I loved her, and always would—I sort of clammed up.'

'It wasn't about that, that I wanted to see you,' Willow quickly inserted. The request she had to make was burning her tongue but then she was suddenly struck by the dreadful haggard look of him. She knew then that she was not the only one at Broadhurst to spend a fretful night, and a question she had not intended to ask, escaped, and gently, she enquired, 'How did things go between you and Gypsy?'

'Don't ask,' he replied fretfully. 'Things couldn't be worse—though Gypsy did seem pleased to see me to begin with. We went out to dinner, and . . .' He paused as though to get himself together, then found a smile when he said, 'Once I get started I shall be here all day.' He then noticed that Willow looked to be fairly strung up too, and he forgot his own problems for a moment, to ask, 'Was it to see if we could forget about the pretence of you being Gypsy, that . . .?'

'Well, there is that too,' Willow butted in. 'More particularly though, I need a lift to Stanton Verney—Ryden has refused.'

That she had just asked Noel to take her to Stanton Verney, seemed to have passed him by. 'Oh, Lord,' he said, 'we'll have to keep up the pretence if he's still being sticky with you. He's really on my side, isn't he?' he added with a worried frown. 'He'll ruin everything between Gypsy and me if he gets half a chance, I know he will.'

'I'm sure you're exaggerating,' Willow said faintly, not at all as sure about that as she would have him believe.

Wearily, as though to say he no longer knew whether he was standing on his head or his heels, Noel shook his head. But when he looked into Willow's sad eyes, he manfully came away from his own perplexities, to enquire, 'Is it because this—business—is making you unhappy, that you want to go home?'

'Will you take me?' she asked, not wanting that anyone should delve into the reasons for her unhappiness. She then found that, when put to the test, Noel was real dear.

He apparently did a quick mental flip through his work load that day, then told her, 'I've a few appointments I made yesterday for this morning which I can't put off but I can get back here for around two, if that's all right?'

Pure and utter relief washed through Willow. It showed in the smile that lit her eyes and mouth. 'I'll be ready,' she said.

'You know,' said Noel, 'you're a darling—and I don't mean only about keeping quiet. Why wasn't it you I fell in love with?' he asked, as gently, he pressed his lips to her cheek.

A cold harsh voice from the bottom of the stairs, barking, 'I suppose you *do* intend to put in an appearance at your office today?' cut icily through any empathy of the moment.

Willow looked down in time to catch the chilling expression on Ryden's face, before, briefcase in hand, he strode out to his car. She knew then that her decision to leave was the right decision. For, leaving out her own feelings, and be she Gypsy, or just plain Willow Cavendish, from the way Ryden had spoken to Noel just now, her presence at Broadhurst was doing nothing but causing a rift between two brothers who had always been very close.

She had more anxious moments before she could bring herself to tell Mrs Kilbane that she was returning to Stanton Verney. It seemed dreadful, when she had been shown such open-hearted kindness by her hostess, that she should spurn that kindness, by saying that she wanted to leave.

Mrs Kilbane's reaction proved that not only was she warm-hearted and kind, but that also she had seen far more than her guest had realised. Willow had said no more than that her knee was so much improved now, and that Noel was going to take her home that afternoon, when Veronica Kilbane exclaimed, 'Noel— not Ryden?' Then, 'Ah,' she said, and went on to explain how her husband occasionally had a crafty forbidden cigar which he thought no one knew about, and how it had become her habit when she thought everyone was asleep, to creep down to check he had not left a lighted stub laying about. 'When I tiptoed into the library,' she went on, 'I surprised Ryden nursing a large scotch and wearing a look on his face that told me something, which had nothing to do with business, was eating at his heart.'

'I . . . he . . .' Helplessly Willow looked at her, and knew not what she could possibly answer.

'It's all right, Willow,' Mrs Kilbane helped her out. 'You don't have to explain. I'd guessed you and Ryden had had a few words when, after Clifton and I had finished watching television, I found that you'd gone to bed.'

Positively hating to deceive Mrs Kilbane, Willow felt more and more miserable by the second. Though she found some small solace when she saw that the brief conversation she'd had with Ryden after dinner, could, she supposed, be described as them having had a few words.

'If you feel you must go, then I won't try to persuade you against your will,' Veronica Kilbane told her. 'Though I shall look forward to seeing you again when you and Ryden have resolved whatever it is that has made you cross with each other,' she added. Then she smiled, and said, 'Now—to more practical matters.'

The 'practical matters' were in evidence when just after half past two that afternoon, Mrs Kilbane had Noel take out to his car a full-to-overflowing carton of fresh provisions which she insisted Willow would need since she would not be able to collect, and carry for herself, from the village store.

While waiting for Noel to arrive, Willow's thoughts had gone to wonder if Ryden's mother suspected she was in love with Ryden. Then, when insisting that she take the walking stick with her too, she came to the car with her, Willow had no doubt that, though she could trust her to keep it to herself, Mrs Kilbane knew. The older woman's look was affectionate when she gave her a hug and kissed her goodbye. She then stood back, and with a wealth of total understanding underlying her words, she whispered, as though it was their secret, 'Come back—as soon as you can, my dear.'

Willow knew she would never again set foot inside Broadhurst Hall, and feeling choked up inside, she was glad that Noel, as she had thought he might, kept up a running commentary about Gypsy the whole way to Stanton Verney.

When it was obvious to her that he was so mixed up he did not know where he was at, she started to give him directions to her cottage.

Noel gave her a rueful grin, and told her, 'I'll admit that the old head was thumping more than somewhat the last time I was in your home but I think I can just about remember where you live.'

He then proceeded to drive straight to her cottage, and proved himself thoughtful when he first assisted her out from his car and indoors and then went back for the groceries, and carried them through to her kitchen.

'Can I make you a cup of tea?' he then offered.

'Not for me,' Willow declined, 'But if you'd like one . . .'

Noel shook his head. 'I must get back.'

'I've interrupted your work,' Willow began apologetically.

'It's the least I can do.' He smiled and confessed, 'Actually, Gypsy's working in town from today until Saturday.'

'And you're seeing her tonight?' she guessed.

'That's right,' he agreed, but started to look worried again. 'Sometimes I can't help wondering if it wouldn't be better if I didn't take a leaf out of Ryden's book, and played it cool. It seems to make his women come running, at any rate.'

Willow did not want to know about Ryden and his women friends. She had been through enough emotional torment and did not require the new emotion of jealousy to give her a battering.

'You're two different types,' she told Noel. 'What might work for Ryden, might not work for you.'

'You're probably right,' he agreed. 'Besides which, there's this need inside me to see Gypsy every day.' He sighed as a thought struck him, 'Not that I'll get the chance next week. I'm off to France on Sunday night.'

'Monsieur Ducret is well again?' Willow pulled the name out of her memory with the hope that a change of subject might take Noel's mind away from his inner unhappiness.

'He's much improved and is, apparently, defying anybody to keep him in bed.'

Willow knew the feeling. The change of subject was to be brief though, for with a look to his watch, Noel was heading for the door. From there he found a smile, and before he left, he told her 'I'll be in touch.'

She doubted that he would. Already his head would be full of Gypsy. And, save for his work, there would be no room for anyone or anything else.

Prior to her 'holiday' Willow had spent a busy life where some days flew by so fast, that there never seemed to be a spare moment. Now, still largely invalided, even if she was getting around more easily, each hour seemed to take an eternity to pass.

At nine that night, feeling more incapacitated by her love for Ryden than by her injury, she went to bed. It had been her hope to have an early night and catch up on some of the sleep she had missed the previous night but an hour later, Willow had not closed her eyes for so much as a cat nap.

When the telephone downstairs rang, she let it ring. She was not expecting anyone to 'phone, and there seemed little point to struggle out of bed, only to answer a wrong number. The 'phone continued to ring though, and refused to be ignored, so she left her bed and made her slow careful way down the stairs.

The 'phone was still clamouring, to tell her that whoever it was at the other end, they were not a type who gave up easily, when she limped across her sitting-room floor.

Typically, though, no sooner had her hand gone out to the offending instrument, than the ringing stopped. All the same she lifted the receiver. As expected, she got the dialling tone. Willow limped to the kitchen and satisfied her boredom by making a cup of tea for which she had no real appetite.

Wednesday dawned bright and beautiful. Willow was unimpressed. For the pure hell of it she had a bath, then spent long painful minutes in getting out from the tub—at the same time she tried not to remember how Ryden had extricated her from the tub the last time she had chosen to live so dangerously, and what had followed.

Damn him, she fumed, when at last, dressed, she made her way down the stairs. It did no good to try and whip up anger against him, she found, for just as thoughts of him would not go away, neither would the love she felt for him depart.

She was nearer to the 'phone this time when it rang. And she felt quite calm when she picked it up and gave her number—until she heard Ryden's voice! For a moment, as her insides started to churn, she thought that, with him so much on her mind, she must be imagining that it was his voice. But there was no imagining the toughness of him that came through when he spoke.

'I suppose you think you've been very clever to act behind my back?' he barked. Her powers of comprehension taken from her in the shock of hearing him, Willow had not an idea of what he meant. 'Even while I was saying you were going nowhere until *I* said so, you had it all planned in your scheming head,' he accused.

Rapidly, Willow came away from her shock and into comprehension. She felt like weeping that his only reason for calling was to give her a piece of his mind that she had put one over on him but nevertheless she drummed up enough aggression to fire back. 'You've known I was a schemer from the very beginning, so why start complaining now?' And, since her telephone number wasn't in the directory, 'How did you get my number?' she charged.

'As you so rightly said,' Ryden tossed back, 'I've have had your number for a long time.'

Willow would have put the 'phone down there and then, only Ryden had not finished speaking, and, idiot that she knew herself to be, she still wanted to hear him.

'Where were you last night?' he bluntly asked. And when she was not quick enough to answer, 'You were out with my brother,' he said, his tone full of accusation—and hate.

It was his hatred, that made her come out fighting—rather that than go under. A fresh shock hit her that, by the sound of it, it had been Ryden who had hung on to that telephone and let it ring and ring last night. She could no longer calmly stand there and take his hate.

'Who says we were out?' she snapped, her pride and self-preservation in uproar. Then, with the thought fresh in her mind of how Ryden, although he did not know it, had got her out of bed to answer the 'phone she gritted, 'There are some moments in a girl's life, when the last thing she has on her mind, is to get out of bed to answer the 'phone.'

She was still hearing his outraged roar seconds after Ryden had banged down the 'phone. Quietly, she replaced her own receiver. That, she thought, is one way of saying goodbye forever.

A sob she had not known was on its way, shook her frame. Promptly then, Willow burst into tears.

CHAPTER NINE

By the time Friday arrived Willow had accepted that, whatever happened in future years, never could any other holiday turn out to be as disastrous as this one.

She freely admitted that she had been so down on occasions this last few days, that at times she had thought never to surface from her utter desolation of spirit. That Ryden hated her, or hated what he believed to be her—he had not bothered to look beyond his wild assumption, which showed how little he really cared—had caused her to hit rock bottom.

But, since the only way out from rock bottom was up, she concentrated all her energies that Friday morning, in looking for plusses. There were no good points to be found in anything connected with Ryden, so first, she must stop thinking about him. Fate gave a hollow laugh.

For a start, she determined, her knee was much, much easier than it had been, so shortly, she would be as nimble footed as she ever was. All she had to do was to survive the weekend, and then, come Monday, her holiday over, she could start picking up the threads of her life.

It seemed a side issue that her knee still objected to any sort of pressure, which meant she might have a problem to drive to work on . . .

Her car! A groan escaped her. Her head had been so full of Ryden, she had just not given a thought to the fact that her car was still in London!

For the best part of the next half-hour, Willow tried to convince herself that she had no need of a car. She was certain it would not worry her if she never saw her car again.

At the end of her stubborn attempt at brainwashing though, she was left with a few obstinate facts. The first of which, since she was as near broke as made no difference, was that to get to her job at Laffard's each day, was a must. Which meant that since Stanton Verney, delightful village though it was, had a bus service that was next to extinct, a car was an essential. Which in turn meant that, however much she did not want to contact Ryden about her car—she would have to!

It was mid-afternoon and Willow had still done nothing about making that contact. She and Ryden had said goodbye and she just did not need to have further hurt inflicted on wounds that had not yet begun to show any sign of healing. She recalled how he had said he would get someone to deliver her car, and, crazy though she knew it, she limped to the window as though by some magic she might see that her car had suddenly materialised.

I am going potty, she thought, when a few moments later, a solution dropped into her head that was so simple, she could not but wonder if having Ryden so constantly on her mind had dimmed her otherwise normal intelligence.

Not long afterwards, she had the number of Kilbane Electronics from Directory Enquiries, and she was busy stabbing out the digits.

'May I speak with Mr Noel Kilbane?' she asked the friendly voice who answered. Then agitation started to bite as she waited in fear that by some mischance, she would be put through to the wrong Mr Kilbane.

Her palms had started to sweat and she was ready to put the 'phone down when she discovered she had been connected correctly. Her luck was out though for Noel's secretary advised her that he was not in his office that afternoon. 'I can take a message if you wish,' she suggested. 'Though his meeting might over-run, when he might not return to his office tonight.'

'I'll—contact him at home,' said Willow, and quickly hung up, knowing that she would do nothing of the sort.

She spent the next couple of hours tying herself in mental knots. Ryden would be going home to Broadhurst that night and since her car was still in London, it was unlikely, in the event of Ryden ever remembering his promise to have her car delivered, that he would take any action about it before nine o'clock on Monday. At nine o'clock on Monday, she had to be at work!

Shortly after seven-fifteen, Willow was again on to Directory Enquiries. Shortly after that, in the hope that Noel had returned to the flat for a wash and brush up before he went to see Gypsy, Willow was once more busy with the digits.

To her tremendous relief, the dialling tone did not go on for very long before the 'phone was answered but her relief went zooming and her palms became moist again when, instead of Noel's voice, she heard a voice she would know anywhere.

'Kilbane,' Ryden repeated, his voice terse this time, a if he was intolerant with fools who rang his number then forgot why they had done so.

'Er ... it's Willow,' she said, wondering at the masochist in her that invited more intolerance, when, had she had time to think, she would, without answering, have put down the 'phone. 'I w-wanted to speak to Noel,' she was forced to go on when nothing but silence came from the other end.

'Impatient for the sound of his voice?' was growled

sarcastically in her ear. Followed by a gritty, 'He cut short a meeting to be in plenty of time for your date.'

'I—expect—he's held up in the Friday night traffic,' Willow replied. Then, her brain starting to wake up, 'Actually—I keep forgetting to ask Noel about my car. I shall n . . .'

'You mean there's *time* for talking when the two of you are together?'

'Goodbye, Ryden,' said Willow, and did not know which one of them put the 'phone down first—though, since he was so good at it, she rather suspected it was him.

Without so much as a 'plan B' to fall back on, Willow went to bed that night none the happier that each time she tried to figure out a way to get to her office on Monday, she drew a blank.

She had still not been able to come up with an answer, when, the following morning, she heard a car pull up outside her cottage. No sooner had she answered a knock on her door, than as well as having the answer, she also had the biggest surprise of her life.

Not only was her car parked right there but also, behind her car, was the car she knew to belong to Ryden—and Ryden, with his eyes on her, was standing beside it!

It had been Noel who had knocked at her door however, and his, 'Hello love,' as he bent and kissed her cheek, was enough to tell her, if she did not already know, that it was important to him that Ryden still believed her to be Gypsy.

'Er—come in—both of you,' she invited, as she took a limped step back and the realisation awakened that, since Noel must have driven her car down, Ryden was here to give his brother a lift, probably to Broadhurst.

Without comment, Ryden walked past her into her

sitting-room. Willow, unable to think of anything much at all, invited both men to sit down.

'Would . . . you like coffee . . . after your drive?' she asked stiltedly, feeling the desperate need to hide in the kitchen until, if fortune smiled, she had found some sort of composure.

'I'll make it,' Noel volunteered cheerfully, to distract her further. 'You must keep off that leg as much as you can,' he added, and appeared as familiar with the geography of her home as if he lived there, a fact not lost on Ryden, she saw, when he frowned darkly as Noel headed for her kitchen. 'You go and sit down. I shan't be a jiff.'

Because there was nothing else for it, Willow went and sat down but, in the constrained moment or two of silence, she knew that Ryden was not too well pleased to be landed with her company.

'How *is* the leg?' he asked, after what seemed an age of nothing being said. 'It's not letting you down, or making its presence felt at inopportune moments, I trust?'

Why was love such a muddle of contradictions, Willow wondered. It seemed such an agony of time since she had last seen Ryden that, with his remark an open reminder of the time in his flat when her injury had brought an abrupt stop to his making love to her, her heart throbbed giddily yet she also felt a return of the urge to bash him over the head with something.

'I manage,' she replied stonily, and was called upon to add nothing more, when Noel poked his head around the door.

'What have you done with the fridge?'

'I haven't got a fridge,' she said without thinking, more than half her thoughts on what a swine Ryden could be without troubling himself too much. She caught his sudden sharp look of puzzlement that, when Noel was such a frequent visitor and must, since her injury, have made her one warm drink if not more, he had somehow never noticed that her kitchen was bare of a refrigerator. 'If you're looking for the milk,' she said, putting a smile into her voice, 'it's on the slab in the pantry where it always is.' As Noel's head disappeared, almost in the same breath, she asked Ryden, 'You didn't go home to Broadhurst last night?'

'That makes two Fridays in a row,' he replied, apparently hell-bent in making her remember the time she had spent in his flat.

'You'll have to take care it doesn't become a habit,' she murmured and glanced from him to smile at Noel who had just come in bearing a tray of coffee.

She was hard put to hold back a darted glance to Ryden when Noel handed her a cup of coffee, and enquired, 'Sugar?' because Ryden knew, while his brother obviously did not, that she took sugar in neither tea nor coffee.

'I'm still watching my waistline for another few weeks,' she murmured, in the hope, when she had the tiniest of waists, that Ryden would think it part and parcel of her job to guard against putting on an ounce of weight. 'What time is your flight tomorrow?' she asked Noel, when frantic for some way to turn the subject, she suddenly recalled he was to fly to France the following evening.

She started to breathe more normally when, his look regretful that he would not see her for a whole week, Noel went into detail about his flight plans, and ended with the promise, 'I've got your 'phone number.'

Willow smiled, and batted away thoughts on how Ryden had her number too. Then Noel, as if to redeem his two slips that could have suggested he did not know her as well as he made out, put down his empty coffee cup and as though he was always putting her car away, said, 'You won't be needing your car this weekend,' a hint there that anywhere they went it would be in his transport, 'I'll garage it for you, shall I?'

'You know where the garage is,' she smiled.

Up until then, she thought she had done rather well in bringing rabbits of conversation pieces out of the hat. But, without Noel there, try as she might to find some neutral topic, her mental processes dried.

'Thank you for arranging with Noel to bring my car,' was the best she could come up with. Ryden gave her a look that said he wanted her thanks for nothing, and a hostile silence looked imminent but instead she found she was gabbling on anyway. 'It's important I have my car for Monday,' she went on, agitated, and wishing that Noel would hurry back. 'What with the village bus service being so poor, I wouldn't have been able to get to work on Monday without . . .'

Ryden's explosive, 'Good God!' had her breaking off to stare at him with startled, uncomprehending eyes. 'You're in no condition to start work yet,' he told her curtly. 'Look at you,' he snarled, his aggressive manner, as always, stirring her to anger. 'You can't even walk without a stick. How the hell do you think you're going to be able to drive, much less stand around all day at some trade fair?'

'I shan't be standing around all day at some trade fair,' Willow replied tartly, angry herself and not so enamoured that he thought his responsibility for her accident should include a right to tell her what she could and could not do.

'No?' He did not believe her for an instant, she knew that. 'Tell me more,' he invited repressively. 'Have you found something more lucrative—something that takes you off your feet perhaps?'

God! Wouldn't she just love to belt him one! 'I shall be doing office work,' she retorted tautly.

'Ye gods,' he sneered. 'What the hell do you know about office work?'

'Enough,' she told him shortly.

'You won't last a day,' was his not so well informed opinion. That was before he sarcastically enquired, 'Who, if he's in his right mind, is taking you on?'

'If you must know, Laffard Fine Porcelain,' she answered, and only just refrained from adding, 'now put that in your drum and bang it.'

Though she had no time to say anything more, for Ryden's overbearing opinion of, 'That'll be the shortest temp job on record,' had just been uttered, when the door opened and Noel came in. Ryden instantly stood up, obviously ready to go and Willow had to do a quick mental flip back to consider if, in her temper, she had said anything that might have let Noel down. Though since Ryden clearly thought it was a temp job she was to start on Monday, and since Gypsy could well take up some temp job until any injury had recovered enough for her to resume her normal work, Willow decided that Noel had not been let down in any way.

'See you later,' said Noel, for his brother's benefit, and for the same reason, giving her cheek a peck.

'Can't wait,' she smiled. Nor could she—to shut the door on the pair of them. She was in love with Ryden again before the purr of his car had gone from her ears.

On Sunday, Willow went to the garage to start up her car. Two minutes later, she limped back inside her cottage. It was annoying to have to admit that Ryden was right, but she had known the moment she had tried to depress the accelerator, and pain had shrieked through her, that she would be driving nowhere tomorrow, or for a good few tomorrows either.

Early that evening, she rang her boss at his home. His

gladness, when he knew it was her, made it obvious that things had not gone too well with her replacement roped in from the invoice typing section.

'Next time you go away on holiday, Willow, please, I beg of you, leave me your holiday address.'

'I'm sure Angela did her best,' she replied, hardly daring to tell him now what she had rung to tell him.

'If that was her best,' he chortled jovially, happy in his mind that Willow would be back to being his secretary on the morrow, and he would not have to suffer Angela for another day, 'then God knows what her worst is like. I was almost driven to put out an S.O.S. on the radio for you. Did you have a nice time, by the way?' he thought to ask.

'Actually . . .' Willow began.

Some minutes later, she replaced the 'phone, and owned to feeling more light-hearted than she had done in what had been an age. It would be good to get back to work.

Mr Beckwith's horror that he might have to put up with the dreaded Angela for so much as one more hour, had been as amusing as his eager readiness to do anything to avoid such a fate. 'I'll come and collect you personally,' he had offered keenly.

True to his word, Samuel Beckwith was at her front door at eight-thirty the next morning, and fussed round her so much, that she had to smile. It was good to be back in harness again but with her work coming easily to her, Willow found that any hope she might have had to be too busy to allow thoughts of Ryden to penetrate, was not to be.

Mr Beckwith was like a dog with two tails to have his right hand sitting across the room from him able to supply him with an instant answer to any question he shot. So the day progressed.

On Tuesday, she was glad to note that although Mr

Beckwith was as attentive as ever to her temporary lameness, his euphoria of the day before, had settled down—or so she thought.

She was still of that opinion though, when around mid-morning, she reached for her stick and told him she needed some paperwork from Sales, and was off for some exercise.

'I'll go,' he said equably, adding that he wanted a personal word with John Taylor, the sales manager, anyway. 'Besides,' he said, as he removed his plump figure from its well dented chair, 'I need the exercise more than you.' He stayed no longer than to ask which papers she wanted, then he was off.

Some time later, however, stuck for the papers he was to bring back, Willow formed the view that she could have been there and back quicker even without the aid of her stick, he had been so long, when Mr Beckwith suddenly breezed in.

'Sorry to be so long,' he apologised, a look of being unusually pleased about something on his face as he placed the papers she was waiting for down on her desk. 'John wasn't in his office.' Willow waited, her look asking to share in why he was looking so tickled to death. 'Though when his 'phone rang, I—er—tried my hand at the customer liaison bit,' he explained vaguely, and though he fairly beamed at her, he left it at that.

Since she knew he wouldn't have been able to keep it to himself had he chanced to take some colossal order over the 'phone, Willow was left to assume that it had amused him that, when he owned Laffard's, he had just played at being the head of one of its departments. Frequently that day though, she caught him looking at her with such a look of high esteem upon his chubby features that she was made to rethink her idea that his pleasure to have her working with him again had in any degree settled.

And it was not only on Tuesday that she caught that same highly-valued glance on her, for they were just packing up for the day on Friday, when she looked up to see he was favouring her with yet another glowing expression. The whimsical thought came that she might ask him for a raise if he did not soon begin to accept that she was back and that she had no intention to take time off and so leave him to the muddle-headed ways of Angela.

On the subject of being muddle-headed though, Willow thought herself *par excellence*. She had spent time enough reliving every word, every nuance, and every look which had come from Ryden, only to grow thoroughly mixed up at the direction in which her thoughts had strayed.

She dwelt on the times when he had not been aggressive with her, and she thought of those moments when he had kissed her and she had known he desired her. Muddle-headed just wasn't a fitting enough description of the way she had gone on to wonder if had he known the truth—that she was not his brother's hard-boiled girlfriend—maybe, in other circumstances, Ryden could have grown to love her a little.

On Saturday morning, Willow resolved, as she did every morning, that she was not going to think about Ryden any more. She then went and had a bath . . .

She cheered up when, her knee now free from its strapping, she discovered that she could comfortably wear trousers again. She was walking much better now, she mused—still on the look out for plusses—and she had not needed to use her stick at all yesterday. Even so, it was carefully that she made her way down the stairs.

She was eating her breakfast when she decided that tomorrow she would have another try to see if she could drive her car. With any luck she might then be able to ring Mr Beckwith, and advise him he would have no need to call and collect her on Monday.

Because she was still not as swift on her feet as normal, her general tidy around that morning took longer than was usual. Just the same though, it was still only ten o'clock when Willow collected her shopping basket and decided to venture to the village shops.

With her basket over her arm, she was about to open her front door, when someone knocking at the other side caused her to almost fall over in her surprise. And that was not her only surprise. For with the door knob still in her hand, when Willow turned it and pulled back the door, she was thrown all of a fluster to find the last man she expected to see, standing there in front of her!

'That was quick,' said Ryden, his eyes fixed firmly on her face, his aggression, notable by its absence.

'I—was—just going out,' said Willow, not all of one piece but still able to glean that his remark stemmed from the prompt way after his knock, the door had opened.

'How's the knee? he enquired, not moving an inch to let her come by.

'Better,' she told him, her head full with wondering as to why he was here. 'Much, much better,' she elaborated. A fear started to grow within her, of what, she knew not, other than that there seemed to be a trace of something in the angle of Ryden's jaw that suggested he had set his mind to something. 'I was just going round to the village shops,' she informed him.

'Stanton Verney is certainly a village of some charm,' he remarked, taking not the smallest notice of her hint that she had no time to stop for a chat.

A chat! Willow caught herself up short. When had Ryden ever made any remark to her that did not have some point! Suddenly, when she knew instinctively that his visit was no social call, her heart began to beat faster. Noel has told him, she thought. Ryden knows the truth! He's come to apologise!

'It is a charming village,' she murmured. She knew without being told that to apologise would not come easy to him, but where she had once savoured the time when this moment would come, now that the moment had arrived, because she loved him, she could just not stop herself from trying to help him out. 'But you haven't come here to pass comments on the village, or to ask about my health, have you, Ryden?' she said gently.

For long moments her heart pounded and Ryden looked at her as if arrested not only by her face, but also by the gentle quality of her tone, time seemed to stand still.

Then, ever the master of the bucket of cold water technique, he pushed a hand carelessly into one pocket, and told her, 'My mother has been most concerned about how you've been coping since you left Broadhurst. I've tried to assure her, of course, that you're quite capable of managing on your own.'

Willow was inwardly calling herself all sorts of names for her idiocy, and, belatedly, recalled that Noel was not due back from France until tomorrow and that, since nothing could yet have been resolved with Gypsy, Noel would not have confessed the truth of the deceit.

Ryden continued, 'My mother wants to see for herself how you are—she would be very pleased if you'd come back with me for morning coffee.'

Startled, Willow stared at him. 'You're—actually—inviting me into your home?' she asked. This definite invitation surprised her, especially as before it had only been his feeling of responsibility for her accident that had persuaded him to take her there.

'I am,' he answered firmly, his grey eyes steady on hers.

But Willow had quickly recovered, and was able to see then that it was not *his* invitation, but an invitation issued by Mrs Kilbane—one which he had delivered purely because of the caring he had for his mother. Pique, an unreasoning pique, hit Willow then, that it was not out of any caring for her that Ryden was there.

'Now isn't that just terrific!' she flared, and in the heat of the moment, she didn't give a tuppenny damn that his eyes had narrowed at her waspish tone. Though she gave him full marks for keeping his cool, when evenly, he replied,

'I'm afraid I don't understand.'

'Not much you don't.' She was suddenly aware that since they were both on the door step, the whole street would hear if, as she felt like doing, she started yelling. 'You know damn well you'd move heaven and earth to keep Noel and me apart, but since Noel is still in France,' she caught his hurriedly concealed flicker of surprise that she had read his mind so quickly, and charged on, 'you thought with him safely out of harm's way, that if to see me would put your mother's mind at rest, then you would grin and bear—just this once—to have my presence in your home.'

'You know, Willow,' said Ryden smoothly, when she had come to a fiery stop, 'you're something of a hothead.'

'Have you only just discovered that?' she snapped.

Strangely then, he smiled, 'I'm discovering more and more about you all the time,' he told her silkily.

She only just managed to bite back the retort that he still had a long, long way to go before he discovered the truth about her. Ryden, however, waited no longer than to see her lips part as though to say something more, and firmly close again, than, urbanely, he continued to bait her.

'I don't appear to have had very much success in keeping you and my brother apart, do I?' and as if not needing an answer he followed on, 'Noel may be on the other side of the channel but I don't doubt that the telephone wires from Paris have been red hot all this week.'

'Is it so unnatural that he should 'phone every day?' Willow said crossly, not happy with lies but too far in now to back out. She saw how unpalatable Ryden found her answer, when he glanced from her to look down to his shoes.

The next second though, his eyes were swiftly back on hers, his stern look telling her he was not going to like any confirming answer she gave, when disagreeably, he asked, 'And I suppose Noel rang you from France last night too?' That niggled Willow—she was past caring what lies she told now—so with a smile she replied, 'He didn't have to. I have his Paris number—I rang him.'

The blatant lie was out but Willow guessed from Ryden's steady considering look, that any second now, he would come back with something short, sharp, and guaranteed to be offensive.

'I must get my shopping done,' she jumped in quickly, in an attempt to avert an insult which could torment her for the rest of the day. 'Would you give Mrs Kilbane my apologies for not joining her for coffee, and tell her,' she rattled on, 'that my knee is no trouble now.' On a sudden thought, she dipped back into a small alcove in the hall, and extracted the walking stick. She handed the stick over to him. 'Your mother will know I've recovered when you give her that,' she told him.

By then, Willow had begun to feel like a piece of

chewed string but Ryden made no move to go to his car and drive off. Still shaken to see him so unexpectedly, she felt unable to keep up her defiant stance for much longer—which left her with no other option, but to take matters into her own hands.

Her shopping basket was still over her arm and, with as much speed as she was capable, she moved and just missed bumping into him when he shifted to one side as she stepped into the street. Firmly then, she pulled the door of her cottage tightly shut.

A mixture of gladness and sadness filled her heart when Ryden went to his car and tossed the walking stick she had given him on to the back seat, and she saw that he had accepted that she was not going to go to Broadhurst with him.

Though when the only reason she could see for him coming back to where she stood, was to bid her a final adieu, she was again shaken when he calmly relieved her of her shopping basket, and, just as calmly, told her, 'I'll give you a lift as far as the shops.'

She was about to argue that she could well walk but got no further than opening her mouth, when her neighbour's door opened, and the only words to leave Willow, as a firm hand caught hold of her arm and propelled her towards and into his car, were, 'G-good morning, Mrs Mason.'

A jumbled up minute followed, while Ryden pulled away from the kerb, in which Willow did not know whom to rail against first: Mrs Mason and her untimely appearance, or Ryden, and his high-handedness.

Her confusion was deepened in that she could not fathom why Ryden was bothering to give her a lift. From the way he had left his keys in the ignition, it was obvious he had only meant his call at her cottage to be a brief one—hopeful of a quick refusal to his mother's invitation he could, duty done, make a fast get away.

Any fresh bewilderment Willow felt when he drove straight past the shops, was to quickly clear when in a very few seconds he turned on to the road that was sign-posted Comberford. Her confusion was then negated by a well-known feeling of frustrated anger against him.

She knew in advance that to order Ryden to stop the car would be a waste of breath, but she was in no mood to take what amounted to kidnapping with any grace.

'Just one cup of coffee,' she stormed as she stared, fuming, through the windscreen, 'then you can jolly well take me straight back to Stanton Verney.'

'Good girl,' murmured Ryden, without heat.

'What's that supposed to mean?' she flared angrily. Too het up to wait for his reply she continued 'That you think just because I can't do anything about it, that I've accepted . . .'

'You may not like to accept it,' he cut in smoothly, 'but I know enough about you to know that once we get to Broadhurst, nothing of what you feel will have you doing anything that might upset my parents.'

At any other time, Willow might have been thrilled to hear the faint suggestion of a compliment coming from him. But, she supposed it must be her defence mechanism acting up again, for hotly, the words spilled from her, 'You think you know *anything* about me?'

'Like I said,' Ryden told her, a tough tone starting to creep into his voice, 'I'm discovering more and more all the time.' That, along with the tone of his voice, had her quiet for half a second and he deliberately changed the subject, to ask, mildly, 'How did the temp job go last week?'

Forced to change her direction of thought, Willow had not forgotten his opinion that she would not last as much as one day.

'Contrary to your most *unvalued* opinion,' she told him sweetly, 'Mr Beckwith, who just happens to be the owner of Laffard Fine Porcelain, was so pleased with the work I did, that he's asked me to stay on for another week.'

Talk about falling on deaf ears, she fumed, when instead of eating craw, all Ryden replied, was, 'I expect he's glad of any pair of hands.' And while she wasn't certain that she would not be hitting him yet, went on, 'Is his usual—er—clerk, or whatever, on holiday?'

'It's the time of the year for holidays,' she answered woodenly.

'Do you like temp work?' he asked as they turned into the drive of Broadhurst Hall.

'I prefer my work at trade fairs,' she lied, not knowing the first thing about such work.

Ryden stopped the car, looked at her as though to say, of course you do, then he got out from behind the steering wheel, and came round to assist her out.

Willow tried to shake off the firm grip he had on her elbow as he escorted her into the house but, as if he suspected that, there under protest, she might run away before she had seen his mother, his hold refused to be shaken. He was determined, it seemed, that she was not going to run away anywhere.

Aware that he was never going to know what his touch could do to her anyway, Willow accepted that she could not shake off his hand and tried to concentrate, as Ryden guided her along the hall and to the drawing-room, on composing her features so that Mrs Kilbane would not know that she was not there voluntarily.

Ryden still had a tight hold on her when at the drawing-room door he halted to turn the handle and push the door inwards. Then Willow too, was pushed forward, and suddenly great clamouring warning bells were going off in her head. For although there was someone taking their ease in the drawing-room, that someone was not Mrs Kilbane!

'That 'phone call you asked me to wait in for didn't . . .' Noel turned in his seat, '. . . come,' he ended, his eyes shooting from Willow to his brother.

'I—thought you were—in—France!' Willow gasped, feeling suddenly stifled when Ryden closed the drawing room door with a determined click and, only then, let go of her arm.

Stupefied, she followed Noel's eyes as he looked to her, then again to his brother, though what Noel read and, knowing Ryden better than she, understood from the no-nonsense look he was wearing, she did not know.

All at once Noel was on his feet, and with his eyes still on Ryden, he quietly told her, 'The French trip was put off again when Monsieur Ducret suffered a relapse.' And while Willow stared at him open mouthed, 'I haven't been out of England all this week,' he informed her.

'You—haven't b . . .' she started to croak, witless for the moment. She was acutely conscious of Ryden standing by her side. Suddenly her stunned brain stirred itself to recall that not too long ago, she had distinctly told Ryden that, only last night, she had telephoned through to Paris and had spoken with Noel!

It was her turn then to switch her gaze to Ryden. Had there been any thought in her that he might have forgotten that most blatant of lies, then just one glance at his set expression, was all she needed to know that Ryden had forgotten nothing and that he was not at all thrilled that he had been lied to.

'Perhaps one of you,' he said, with a mildness of tone she suddenly had no belief in, 'wouldn't mind telling me—what in *hell's* name is going on?'

CHAPTER TEN

ONLY the loud tick of the drawing-room clock, never before noticed by Willow, infiltrated the taut silence that followed Ryden's too mild request.

It was fully evident that he had discovered *something*! Whatever he knew, or had guessed at, Willow had an idea that he would settle for nothing but the whole truth and in her view, the truth should come from Noel.

'Well?' Ryden barked, his aggression starting to rear when neither she nor Noel had said a word.

'It wasn't all Noel's fault,' she spoke up, the tension getting to her when Noel stubbornly remained silent.

Bravely she weathered the glint that came to Ryden's eyes that she had taken it upon herself to defend his brother. She might have gone on to tell Ryden that some of the fault had to be his, too. Had he allowed her to get a word in edgeways at his flat to tell him she was not his brother's girlfriend, then the deception would never had got underway. She was however, suddenly struck by the thought that as Noel was saying nothing, he might still be hopeful of carrying on with the deception!

Ryden had grown impatient of the two of them. He rounded on her, naturally not understanding how half the fault could be his.

'So you openly admit half the blame is yours?'

'None of this is Willow's fault,' Noel broke his silence to interrupt. Ryden however, seemed not to care to have Noel defend her; any more than he cared to have Willow defend his brother. Noel got no further than, 'She . . .' when he was abruptly chopped off.

'Just how many girlfriends do you run at one and the same time?' Ryden demanded furiously without waiting for his answer. 'Did he propose to you too, as well as his other girlfriend—Gypsy?' he blazed at Willow.

It completely passed Willow by that Ryden had just declared that he knew she and Gypsy were two different people for she was not thinking, but feeling. To hear that Ryden was so uncaring of her, that it mattered not a damn to him in his search for the truth that she might be hurt to know that Noel had proposed to someone else, hit at the heart of her.

If she had been blind to what had been revealed then Noel was not.

'You—know—that Willow—is not Gypsy?' he asked incredulously.

'Of course, I know,' Ryden snarled, as though he thought Noel was an idiot. 'I've known for days.'

'You've—left it until *now*—to say something?' Noel exclaimed and still sounding amazed, 'That's not like you! I'd have thought you'd come gunning for me the moment you found out?'

'To hear more lies?' Ryden scorned. 'I wanted the two of you together,' he rapped. 'Today had been my first opportunity.'

Shaken, her intelligence started to come alive, 'You set us up!' Willow gasped.

'*I* set *you* up!' Ryden roared, his aggression on the loose. 'What in God's name, do you think the two of you did to *me*?'

'You deliberately led me on to say I'd telephoned Noel in Paris,' Willow flared, coming away from her hurt, Ryden's aggression, as ever, arousing out her own. 'Mrs Kilbane never did invite me over for coffee, did she?' she challenged hotly. And, when his only answer was a cold look she remembered how he had left his car keys in the ignition when he had called at her cottage.

'You were determined to get me here one way or the other,' she flew. 'If need be, to drag me screaming to your car—you were all ready for a fast take off, weren't you?'

'If needs be,' he did not deny. 'It wasn't in my mind to give either of you another chance to plot and scheme what to tell me behind my back.'

At his words 'plot and scheme' all heat left her—to be replaced by hurt. Even though he knew she was not the girl he had thought she was, his opinion of her was still no better. Left in no doubt that he thought her no better than Gypsy, Ryden then proceeded to put the last nail in the coffin of her foolish hopes that when he knew the truth, perhaps he might see her in a better light.

As he looked from one to the other, it was bitingly that he ground out, 'And now—I want the truth. I want to know why the deception—why the lies?' His tone was little short of murderous and Willow received the full glare of his eyes, when he snarled, 'I want to know exactly what goes on between the two of you.'

She had thought she had known all about the pain of loving unwisely but it was quite obvious that even though Ryden knew she was not Gypsy, his hatred of her, too, was such that he positively loathed any suggestion that there was anything at all going on between her and his brother. The ache within her was more than she could take.

Were it not for the fact that she was not as fast on her feet as she would like to be, Willow would have run from the room and left Noel to explain all he wished. She was still there, however, when Ryden, totally infuriated by the non-answers he was getting, confirmed that he still thought her the dregs of humanity.

'I want to know where Gypsy fits into all this, and if it's she my brother plans to marry. Or,' he said fiercely, his face white in his loathing, 'if he thinks I'll stand calmly by, and let him marry you!'

That Ryden should not hesitate to let his hate of Willow Cavendish be known, had Willow crucified with deep pain. Tears, as yet inside, had begun to surge upward. No way could she take that final hurt.

Giving not a second's thought to the fact that only yesterday had she abandoned the aid of her walking stick, she took off. The pain in her knee was as nothing compared with the pain that racked inside. Tears she could no longer hold in, rained down her face as she sprinted for the outside door. Vaguely she was conscious of a shout, a commotion, behind her, but she was bleeding inside and wished, as she slammed the outside door hard shut, that she could so easily slam the door shut on all she was feeling.

There was only one car on the drive but she cared not whose car it was. All she knew was that she had to put some distance between her and Broadhurst with all speed.

Without knowing how she knew, she was aware that Ryden had again left his keys in the ignition. In a pain filled world, Willow was behind the wheel and had the car in motion before she had the door closed.

More pain stabbed from within when she saw Ryden bolt from the house and yell something as she sped past him. All he cared about was that she was pinching his car, damn him—she hoped she crashed it.

A mile down the road, pain in her knee separated itself from the pain in her heart, and forced her to pull over. A sob shook her when, defeated, she rested her head on the steering wheel.

She had no time in which to collect her thoughts, or in which to give any consideration to what she had just done, for, all at once, the sound of someone driving a car like a maniac hit her ears. Though she might well have ignored the sound, the squeal of tyres on tarmac told her that the car had come to a sudden stop somewhere nearby and she could not ignore that in the next moment the driver's door of the car she was in, was wrenched open!

Nor could she ignore that Ryden, still white faced, and still furious, was striving to get on top of some emotion, when on a strangled kind of breath, he said, 'Don't you *ever* dare do that to me again.' Willow stared at the ravaged look of him. 'Are you hurt? You must be, you're crying . . .' he demanded.

'Leave me alone,' Willow snapped, even as beaten as she felt, some inner instinct refused to let anyone else know it. 'Why don't you just clear off?' she said rudely, brushing away her tears of hurt with the back of her hand. 'I'll return your car when . . . You can take it now,' she changed her mind, 'I'll walk home.'

'Don't be so bloody stupid!' Ryden exploded. 'You're not walking anywhere. In fact,' he told her, at his charming worst and yet starting to look tough again, 'you're going nowhere until you and I have got a few things said.'

From Willow's point of view, she had heard more than enough, but still she was not prepared to show her defeat.

'What!' she feigned surprise. 'Didn't Noel tell you *all*?'

'I didn't wait to hear anything . . .' Ryden began grimly, his impatience becoming more evident. 'Are you going to let me in, or do I cut my way through the hedge you've parked bang up against, to get into the passenger seat?' he said aggressively.

She had been careless as to how close to the hedge she had stopped and closed her mind to the few scratches the car's paintwork had probably picked up. She saw that as she obviously wasn't going anywhere until he said so, she might as well move over, the quicker to have it all done.

'Now,' said Ryden quietly, once his long length was inside the car beside her, 'would you mind telling me exactly what all that was about?'

Willow knew full well what he was asking, but she wished he had stayed aggressive. For, just the fact that along with his quiet tone, his belligerence had quieted, made her own animosity difficult to find.

She had no wish to tell him anything but Ryden now seemed to have all the patience in the world. He looked as though he was prepared to sit there until midnight, or for however long it took before she did make some reply. She shrugged carelessly.

'What does it matter? I'm not going to marry your brother—even if he asks me, which he won't.'

The sound of Ryden's sudden sucked in breath made her turn her head. His colour, she saw, was coming back.

'It matters, a very great deal,' he replied, but Willow looked away from him and beat back fresh waves of hurt. She already knew how it mattered to him that she did not marry Noel.

What she did not know though, was why, now that he was in receipt of the knowledge that she was not likely to be his sister-in-law, Ryden had made no move to start the car to return her to Stanton Verney?

'Can we go now?' she asked, dry eyed but with the need to let go and have a jolly good howl still prodding her.

'Perhaps you didn't hear what I said,' he replied. She had not forgotten a syllable but he nevertheless reminded her, 'We're going nowhere, until we've got a few things said.'

Hemmed in as she was, Willow gave him a frustrated glance. 'Say all you want,' she gave him the floor. 'But, for the record,' she tossed in, 'I'm not interested in a word of it.'

'There are times, Willow Cavendish,' Ryden retorted threateningly, 'when I could cheerfully wring your slender neck.'

'Put the boot in,' she invited carelessly—he had all but finished her off anyway. She had the ominous feeling that whatever he had to add, might just about complete the job.

'You sound,' he said slowly, 'as though I've . . . hurt you, in some way.'

Her breath caught; in her attempt to be off-handed, she had tripped herself up. Pride made her tell him airily, 'Think nothing of it.' All at once though, that indifferent tone deserted her and left her totally without cover. She said tartly, 'I don't know what you think I am but to hear that *any* man has such a low opinion of me that nothing would induce him to stand calmly by and let his brother marry me—did damn well hurt.'

'My God!' Ryden sounded appalled. 'Is that why you lit out as though . . .?'

'No, no of course not,' Willow furiously denied. Too late though, she saw she had revealed far, far, too much. Suddenly, she did not know where on earth she was, because Ryden's left arm had come about her shoulders, and gently, he laid a kiss to her cheek.

Abruptly she pushed him away. 'So now you've kissed it better,' she said, a riot of agitation within her, even as he took his arm from her shoulders. 'I want to go home. I've an awful lot to do today,' she added as an afterthought. 'And——'

'Willow Cavendish,' said Ryden grimly, cutting through what she had been about to say. 'I have not endured days . . . no, weeks,' he contradicted, 'of not knowing where the hell I'm at. So don't think that just because you're nervous of what any conversation we have might reveal, you can avoid that conversation.'

'I—don't understand you,' she mumbled. One half of her was panic-stricken that he had seen how nervous she was in her fear that she might slip up and reveal that it was not just *any* man's low opinion of her that hurt—while the other half of her could not deny being intrigued to know, when she had always thought Ryden supremely confident in all he did, why he should have spent weeks, in not knowing where the hell he was at!

'There were too many things I didn't understand either,' he acknowledged. 'To start with, having formed a definite opinion of the wretched woman Noel had been so distressed about when I 'phoned him from the States, no sooner had I met you, than I was seeing a person who didn't in any way, shape or form, jell with that opinion.'

'I tried to tell you—in your flat—that I wasn't Gypsy,' Willow, when she had not meant to say another word, found herself saying.

'I've wondered about that,' he told her. 'God, how you tolerated the overbearing swine I was to you then, I shall never know.'

That Ryden was sounding more friendly than aggressive, cheered her and she almost found a smile, when she told him, 'There were times when I'd have loved to have taken a swing at you—if I'd been capable of standing without losing my balance.'

'You were so brave and all I did was lay into you,' said Ryden gently.

A dreamy smile started somewhere inside Willow to have Ryden this gentle with her, when for most of the time, it was his aggression she was more familiar with. The dreamy smile did not make it. Sirens suddenly sounded in her head as it dawned on her that, if he carried on this way, she would soon be quite defenceless!

'Is that it then?' she asked brightly. At his short look of surprise she went on, 'Was that our little talk? I must get some tomatoes before the shops cl . . .'

Summarily he sliced her off, the old aggression returned and banished his gentleness when he charged, 'Did anyone ever tell you, that you are, without a doubt, the most frustrating female in all the world?' He sounded as frustrated by her as he had intimated. 'I'll let you know when this conversation is over,' he curtly told her.

It was clear to Willow that he was determined to have this talk with her but, since any non-aggressive comment he made seemed to winkle out a softness in her, she decided to stay mute.

'As I was saying . . .' he continued, when a few minutes had elapsed whilst he overcame the frustration she aroused in him. 'I met you and, when my preformed opinion of you didn't jell, I concluded that naturally, you'd have to be something of an actress too. It was only when I put together two or three incidents—isolated at the time—that a picture started to emerge, and I saw that Noel's girlfriend Gypsy, was a very different person from the girl I knew as Willow Cavendish.'

More determined than ever not to say a word, Willow stayed silent. Her heart fluttered to hear that Ryden had thought to question anything about her, isolated incidents, or otherwise. Much though she would have preferred that his slighting comments back at Broadhurst had killed her love for him stone dead she realised that her love was still alive. She was as much in love with him as ever.

'But . . .' said Ryden, and then paused.

Willow, curious, looked up at him. Grey eyes stared

back at her, determined grey eyes that endorsed his intention to get some reaction from her unspeaking frame. He refused to let her look away and resumed, 'But it wasn't until Tuesday, that the picture became much, much clearer.'

Still Willow said not a word. She was sure she just did not want to hear any of this but since she could go nowhere, she sat with stubbornly compressed lips.

She kept up her intransigent stance until Ryden, looking straight at her and nowhere else, remarked, almost casually, 'On Tuesday—I rang Laffard Fine Porcelain.'

For all of two seconds, her response was a stunned non-reaction, then, still absolutely flabbergasted she hoarsely croaked, 'You—rang—my firm?' What he had done hit home. Suddenly her reaction was one of immediate boiling anger. 'You had the *nerve*,' she shrieked, 'to ring and ask questions about me? Last Tuesday!' she yelled, as it penetrated that Laffard's could have been a hot bed of gossip about her for the past four days and that she had never known. 'Who did you speak to?' she demanded. She wondered how she would ever dare to show her face at work again if he had been quizzing the blabber-mouthed girl who operated the switchboard.

To her further humiliation, however, she discovered that Ryden had not been satisfied with any one but the top man.

'He introduced himself as Samuel Beckwith,' he told her, coolly. She was fuming. 'You reminded me of his name,' he murmured with honeyed tones, 'when on our way to Broadhurst, you said how pleased Mr Beckwith was with your work that he had asked you to stay on for another week.'

Warm colour flushed her cheeks that Ryden had known *on that drive* that she was lying through her teeth. If he had 'phoned Mr Beckwith, and she did not doubt that he had, then she could be quite certain that Ryden had known since last Tuesday, that her work at Laffard's was no temp job.

'How dare you?' she cried, immediately back on the attack. 'How *dare* you ring my boss to ask questions about me?'

'Your employer was most obliging with his information about you,' Ryden came back evenly. 'As far as I remember though, I asked him nothing.'

'Blow that for a tale!' Willow snapped. Curiosity stirred in her again and peaked as, not reiterating what he had just said, Ryden instead left it to her to work it out for herself. 'You must have asked him *something*,' she said, after a moment or two. 'No one just answers the 'phone, and then gives forth about his secretary.'

She bit her lip as her position in the Company slipped out, and hated Ryden when the corner of his mouth quirked as though he had controlled what might have been a smile.

'That's true,' he agreed. And, carefully, it seemed to her, so that if she'd had time she might have wondered why he was being so cagey, he told her, 'I rang, for the purpose of—acquiring a few pieces to decorate some of the outer offices at Kilbane Electronics.' Already she was mentally questioning, would he do such a chore personally and why choose Laffards? 'It occurred to me that the reception rooms could do with a more cheerful appearance. However,' he went quickly on, 'my call was routed to a man who, no sooner had I stated my business, and requested a Laffard Collection catalogue, very genially introduced himself and said that while he owned the company, he was very pleased he had been in the Sales Department to take my call in the sales manager's absence. He then asked who it was who had put me on to Laffard Fine Porcelain.'

Inwardly groaning, Willow saw it all. Mr Beckwith kept abreast with things in the business world. He would recognise the name Kilbane Electronics as being a top notch company, straight away. No wonder he had been tickled pink when he had come back from the Sales Department after taking Ryden's call last Tuesday. No wonder he had looked at her so often ever afterwards with that highly-esteemed look. He would have been puffed up with pride that, even though there were many other, more well-known, high class producers of fine porcelain around; none other than the head of Kilbane Electronics had been in touch, *personally*, with him.

'You told him it was me, who'd mentioned Laffard's to you?' she asked, but she already knew the answer.

'I told him I knew a Miss Cavendish, whom I believe was doing a temp job somewhere in his firm,' Ryden replied.

Oh, grief, Willow thought, wondering how she was ever going to look her boss in the eye on Monday. 'Er—Mr Beckwith—he told you that I wasn't doing a temp job?' she asked faintly, aware she was going to have to face up to where her lies had got her.

'I was, to put it mildly, quite surprised,' he murmured, 'to learn that, not only were you his most valued personal secretary, but also that you'd been with the company since you left college.'

'It—um—must have been something of a surprise,' she mumbled.

'At first, I couldn't believe it. I knew full well you were employed by some agency or other.'

'But—Mr Beckwith, he made you believe it?' she asked, wanting to die with the embarrassment of it all.

'Oh yes, he made me believe it,' said Ryden, his look quiet on her embarrassed face. 'I knew there was no mistake when he went on to tell me how absolutely floundering he'd been without you, his right hand, while you were away on holiday. And, how horror struck he'd been that he might be without your efficient self for another couple of weeks, when you rang him on Sunday to say how you'd sprained your knee and couldn't drive your car.'

'He's—er—been chauffeuring me to and from work all this week,' Willow put in, feeling the need to say something. Though at the nod of Ryden's dear head—she no longer hated him—she saw he already knew that.

'He was glad to do it,' he commented. 'In fact, he seemed a happy man all round . . .' Ryden paused, then with his eyes still on her, he continued, '. . . until—still winded by what I'd so far heard—I put the suggestion that if you worked for him permanently during the day, and since I couldn't believe I'd got you mixed up with another girl whom I knew worked the trade fair circuit, that perhaps you did exhibition work in the evenings.'

Willow knew what was coming. One could not spend five days a week working with someone one liked, without conversation entirely unconnected with work entering into the day somewhere. Besides which, on those occasions towards the end when she had wanted an hour off or sometimes longer, she had told Mr Beckwith why she needed to be at home with Mrs Gemmill.

'He told you about Mrs Gemmill, didn't he?'

'He did,' Ryden agreed, a curiously gentle note coming to his voice. He went on, 'He also told me how, when you finished your stint for the day as his secretary, you would race home to nurse the old lady you'd lived with ever since your mother had gone to live abroad. And how you had your hands too full in tending and caring for Mrs Gemmill to have any free time to *visit* any trade fair, much less to work at one.'

Sadness, from still missing her old friend, touched

Willow. 'Mrs Gemmill died at the beginning of May,' she said quietly, though she rather thought he knew that too.

'And you moved out when the avaricious relatives landed,' he stated, understanding added to that still curiously gentle tone.

Willow coughed to clear a suddenly choky throat. 'True,' she said on a bright note that didn't fool anybody. 'I was exceptionally lucky to find the cottage.' She gabbled on quickly. 'Not that it's big enough for more than one, which is probably why it wasn't snapped up before.'

'Which explains,' said Ryden, appearing to go along with her chirpy manner, 'why you haven't got a flatmate.'

'Ah-h,' said Willow, her bubble of brightness pricked. 'Was that the first thing that didn't jell?' she asked, remembering that he had been about to dump her, when she had revealed that she had no flatmate.

'Because of the fact that it was an accursed nuisance since I was going to have to do something else with you,' he owned honestly, 'I didn't take too much notice of it at the time.'

'Don't spare me,' she said shortly. She had known all along how it was with him but somehow, during the last few minutes, she had lost sight of that.

Strangely then, Ryden breathed, 'Oh Willow, Willow, have you no idea . . .?' Abruptly, he broke off, and she was not sure then as she stared at him, that a hint of dull colour had not come up under his skin.

She knew she must be mistaken, however. Having experienced the most giddy of feelings to hear him, almost tenderly, breathe her name, she was at pains to find the contrariness that had risen in her nature.

'I'm sure I have *every* idea,' she snapped. 'You came after me just now purely and simply because *your* plots and *your* schemes to confront Noel and me, came unstuck when I ran off.'

'I came after you,' Ryden retorted crisply, 'because I was terrified you would kill yourself before . . .'

'Before you could do it for me,' Willow cut in hotly. Then—catching up with what he had just said, 'You-you—were—*terrified*?' she asked, startled.

He nodded. But he seemed then as if he didn't know what to say next or, if he knew, was lost to know where to begin. That to Willow's mind, was surprise enough, for *never*, when it came to saying anything to her, had Ryden ever been struck for words!

Whatever else she had been expecting him to say though, she was left gaping and very nearly floored when, the frustration in him obviously coming to a peak, he suddenly burst out in exasperation, 'Dammit, woman, you're driving me out of my head!'

For once, the aggression in her, that was usually so seldom backward to meet his head on, refused to surface. As she stared at him, so she began to perceive that there was some other emotion lurking behind his irascible front. She was suddenly too jittery to try to put a name to that emotion, but something inside of her was pushing her and was refusing to let her take refuge behind some trite remark.

'I—don't—quite understand, how?' she said, a huskiness in her voice over which she had no control.

Her throat dried up altogether when, her glance momentarily caught by his distracted movement, she looked to where his hands now rested on the steering wheel and she saw that his hands—were shaking!!

She had done no more than send a startled glance to his suddenly tense expression when, as if impatient with himself and impatient with her, Ryden said, 'You know, of course, that I was dead set against you—Gypsy,' he corrected, and twisted round impatiently to face her full square, 'before I had ever met Noel's—lady-love.'

'I soon learned that,' she quietly confirmed.

'What you—don't know about,' he went on, after some seconds of hesitation, 'is the battle that waged in me not to like—and admire—the blonde-haired, green-eyed beauty, who was helpless in my flat.'

'You—started t-to like . . . to admire me?' Willow asked jerkily. She was sure repudiation was on its way, and thought to hurry it—the quicker for her feet to return to earth. 'You could have fooled me,' she started to bite. 'My memory of that time at your flat is that . . .'

'I was little short of a bear with a sore head for most of the time,' Ryden filled in for her. He went swiftly on, 'How else could I be? I'd never known Noel be so demented as he was when he told me of the heartless way that woman had rejected his marriage proposal.'

'So—as soon as I told you Noel had left the flat key behind at my place—you decided I was Gypsy, and—hated me?'

Ryden nodded. Her heart sank—but then Willow found herself on an emotional see-saw when he said, 'The very next morning, I had evidence that I did not hate you as much as I thought I did.'

'You discovered I'd had an accident,' said Willow, and did not know quite where she was any more.

'And was furious about it,' he admitted. 'I was certain your physical suffering was no more than you deserved for the mental suffering you had caused Noel. I was to realise, however, when you said "That should please you" in answer to my question of was your knee hurting like hell—that, it did *not* please me to have you suffering pain.'

'Oh . . .' Willow murmured, any thinking power she had, gone completely.

'It was "oh" too,' he said. 'In next to no time, desire

for you had made itself felt in me. Which,' he went on, 'had me desperately trying to fight the attraction of you—because I knew it would just about finish Noel off, if I ever had to own that I had bedded the woman he loves.'

'It was—probably—propinquity,' Willow found the breath to tell him. 'It was only—physical—after all,' she added haltingly.

'Which is exactly what I told myself,' Ryden agreed. 'Only, I soon found out, it was more than that.'

'Don't . . .' cried Willow in sudden alarm. 'Don't! If—all this, all of what you're saying, is just a punishment for . . .' she broke off, her nerves so jumpy that only when she was half way through, did she realise what she was saying.

Oh God, she thought, when the stilled looked of Ryden told her that his brother had been right about how quickly he could put two and two together. She had not needed to finish what she was saying. Ryden had mentally finished it for her.

'Are you afraid . . .' he began to ask, that calm look still with him when, choosing his words carefully, he continued, 'that if I tell you—what it was I did find out, it might . . .' He paused to take what seemed to her to be a steadying breath. 'That it might be a—a cause for happiness for you—which, could—turn sour and be a punishment, if I don't truly mean, with all my heart and soul, what I'm telling you?'

Abruptly Willow turned her head and faced the side window darkened by the hedgerow, and summoned up coldness from every quarter. Then, with an attempt to freeze off any more questions, icily, she tossed over her shoulder, 'I want to go home.'

How Ryden had taken her frigid request, she was not looking round to find out. No more than five seconds had ticked away, though it seemed like an eternity, when suddenly, she was having to swallow hard for control. All at once, there was a gentle hand on each of her shoulders and, as if his touch was not enough to send jumpy nerves into overdrive, Ryden spoke gently, his voice sounding much nearer to her ear than she had thought.

'You *are* afraid.'

Hastily, she shook her head. 'I'm not,' she denied. 'I'm not.' There was a huskiness in her voice again, that beat away all sight of frost.

'Why then,' he quietly asked, 'when you've never run away from anything in your life—except,' he qualified thoughtfully, 'the recent incidence of you tearing out of Broadhurst because of the hurt I caused you—do you want to go home?'

Of the opinion that she had already said too much, Willow, in the hope that he would get the message and take her home, shook her head to indicate she did not intend to utter another word.

Those gentle hands on her shoulders . . firmed. He turned her round to face him and she was powerless to stop him. She did not want to meet his eyes but when Ryden placed a hand beneath her chin and tilted her head up, she found that there was no way, in the close confines of the car, she could avoid looking straight into his eyes.

His eyes held her. Tenderly Ryden asked, 'Could it be, my dear, dear Willow, that the emotion which revealed itself within me on the day I walked into the drawing-room and found you holding hands with my brother is, dare I hope, reciprocated?'

Oh, help me somebody, she wanted to cry. She wanted to stay, she wanted to run and was, she admitted, never more afraid. Instinct was warning her but of what she was too inwardly stewed up to know.

'What . . .' she began and found she had to clear her

throat again when that word left her on a cracked note. 'What emotion would that be?' she managed to ask without faltering.

She wished that she had not asked at all when, his face was suddenly stern and never more deadly serious. That look forewarned that the big let down, the punishment she had earned, was on its way.

Indeed, so certain of that was she, that she just stared at him uncomprehendingly when Ryden, to the contrary, told her, 'The emotion at the root of the searing jealousy that near destroyed me to see you and Noel holding hands—was love.'

'You . . .' love me, she had been about to add. But so shattered was she at what he had just said, that what she did add, was '. . . were—jealous, of Noel?'

'I don't know how I kept myself from hitting him,' Ryden confessed, his eyes still fast on hers.

'Your father was there,' she reminded him, rather idiotically she thought but since her heart was racing to beat all speed records and her brain power seemed to have scattered to have just heard what she had, that did not surprise her.

'You wouldn't like to put me out of my misery?' Ryden asked but she had no hope of understanding what he meant. When she just solemnly stared he went on, 'The only reason I cannot stand by and let my brother marry you,' he told her, more deadly serious than ever, 'is because I want to marry you myself.'

'Oh!' said Willow on a whispered breath as she wondered if it would help if she pinched herself.

Then, she blinked. All at once, it was as if her vision had cleared to give her fresh insight. Suddenly it seemed to her that Ryden was—more under some terrible strain than deadly serious. As the thought came to her that he looked as if he might start to break if she did not soon give him some concrete evidence of the way things were with her, Willow found herself saying, 'I think that—I should like to marry you, very much. But . . .'

'But, nothing,' Ryden muttered as he let go a pent up breath. 'I've sweated it out for long enough—now, let me hold you.' In the next moment, both his arms were around her, 'Oh God,' he groaned into her hair as he held her close up against his heart, 'I never want to go through a time like that again.'

Just as though he could not believe the time he had spoken of was over, he pulled back so that he could see into her face, and then questioned,

'You *will* marry me? I *did* hear you say you will?'

'Oh yes,' breathed Willow tremulously.

'And—swine though I've been—you do love me a little?' he persisted.

'Do you love me?' Willow asked.

'It's hell, this uncertainty, isn't it?' he said gently. 'Yes, my long suffering little darling, I love you. I love you so much, it's been driving me insane.'

Her smile broke free, 'Oh, Ryden,' she cried, 'I do love you.' Her arms were around him too when their lips met.

Gently, tenderly, at first, Ryden kissed her. And it seemed to her as he broke his kiss to plant tiny kisses over her face, as though he too had been through that dreadful desolation which she had thought would never end.

As he claimed her mouth, and again and again kissed her, each kiss they shared made that loneliness of spirit rapidly recede, and when next Ryden pulled back so he could look into her face, that ache in her heart had gone for ever.

'If I'm dreaming,' she said softly, a warm flush created by his kisses there on her cheeks, 'don't wake me.'

'Have you been through the same hell I've been through, my love?' he asked.

'I loved you, but I thought you hated me,' she said simply.

Ryden traced a feather-light kiss across her brow. Then, as though to protect her from anything that might dare to hurt her, he tucked her head into his shoulder and, with his arms firm about her, he vowed, 'I'll never be unkind to you again.'

'You were a—bit of a brute,' she attempted to tease.

'Don't remind me,' he groaned, Then he confessed, 'I knew, without being aware of what emotion was attacking, that it was not hate I felt when, on that drive down, you casually let out how you didn't have a flatmate.'

'You were furious with me at the time,' Willow recalled.

'I was furious with myself,' he replied, and she heard a self-deprecating smile in his voice, when he added, 'I was furious to discover that I just couldn't dump you at your flat to get on with life. Furious,' he revealed, 'to find, when I believed you deserved no better, that something inside of me just wouldn't let me do that.'

'Oh!' escaped Willow on a sigh as she turned up her head and Ryden bent to salute her lips with his. Then, apparently liking the feel of her head tucked into his shoulder, he settled her there once more.

'I took you into my home determined to throw you out—without mercy—should you upset either of my parents in the smallest degree. And then,' he said, a smile in his voice again, 'I began to discover a new meaning to the word "enigma", because enigma just didn't begin to describe the woman you were turning out to be.'

'Because I wasn't the—bitch—you thought me, to your parents?' she guessed.

'You were perfect to them,' he murmured. 'I now know, I could have saved myself the effort of trying to puzzle out what to make of you—you were just being your natural self with them. Is it any wonder,' he said tenderly, 'that they are both enchanted with you?'

'Your mother . . .' Willow began, then faltered when, her confession of love so recent, she experienced a moment of shyness, 'er—your mother knows that I'm in love with you.'

'She *does*?' Ryden exclaimed, as he moved so he could look into Willow's shy face and, as a fullness of emotion took him because of it, he pulled her yet closer into his protection.

'I didn't tell her,' Willow explained. 'Thinking back though, I think she must have seen love in my joy when you came home from London so unexpectedly . . .'

'You were both in the garden,' said Ryden, on instant recall, and Willow looked up to see him smile as he remembered, 'I didn't see your love, but,' his smile became a positive grin, 'how my heart lifted that you looked pleased to see me. You have no idea, my darling,' he went on softly, 'of the hope, and the fear, that were born when I saw you greet me with a smile.'

'Hope—that I might care?'

'Hope that I might be able to get you to care,' he agreed, 'and fear of what I would have to do to Noel and his heartfelt desire if I was to try to attain *my* heartfelt desire. But,' he solemnly continued, 'things went sour for me that very same night. I felt such a mixture of jealousy and a feeling of frustration that you had begun to feel indifferent to whether I was there or not, that I had to dig away at you to try to get some reaction.'

'You told me I was going nowhere until you said so,' she remembered.

'And just to show me what you thought of that, when I raced down to Broadhurst the next night, I found you gone.'

'You 'phoned me—twice—after that,' she recalled.

'And wished that I hadn't,' he owned. 'The thought of you in bed with Noel was wrecking me,' he said gruffly. 'I decided then that if I was to retain my sanity, I was going to have to follow my own advice to Noel, and cut you out of my mind, and out of my life. Only,' he murmured, planting a gentle kiss to the side of her face, 'it wasn't that easy.'

'Because—I rang to speak with Noel, about my car and you answered?'

'You haunted me day and night without that 'phone call,' he replied. 'When we did deliver your car though, while I saw ample evidence that Noel knew his way around your home, there was also evidence that maybe he didn't know you as well as I'd been led to believe.'

'You—er—noticed his slip—about not knowing I didn't take sugar?'

Ryden smiled. 'Which you covered so well, that it wasn't until later, with you never out of my head, I started to ponder not only about that, but other incidents too. Why, I then asked myself, when according to Noel he was used to shelling out for things the blonde headed Gypsy just had to have—why, when he was a constant visitor, was he not only unaware that you hadn't a fridge, but why hadn't you accepted the gift of a fridge from him? I had a whole weekend,' he told her, 'in which to recall that Noel had at some time definitely told me you had a flatmate. A whole weekend in which to puzzle, why was there not only no flatmate, but, how come you lived not in a flat, but in a cottage?'

'You—um—couldn't find the answers?'

'Not one,' he owned. 'Which had me biting back, several times last Monday, the need to put a few questions to my brother.'

'But instead,' she put in, 'on Tuesday, you rang Laffard's?'

'God knows why. It certainly wasn't in my mind that I'd hear any of what I did hear when I picked up that 'phone. So it must have been,' he said, 'the pure necessity to have some contact with you, however slight, that had me dialling to where I knew you were. Did I have a surprise when, without knowing the reason, I realised just how well and truly I'd been led up the garden path?'

'Were you—angry?'

'To start with, I was so stunned that I only just retained sufficient wit to ask Samuel Beckwith not to tell you I'd 'phone lest, since I'd obviously got you mixed up with some other female, you were offended. Then, having terminated my call, all I could do was sit and stare at the 'phone in my hand. Then, I was at once overjoyed that you could not be Noel's Gypsy, and furious and in a fever of wanting to sort the pair of you out. But,' he said, 'that was all before I got round to thinking about it.'

'And when you did—get round to thinking about it, I mean?'

'Ah,' said Ryden, that smile back in his voice. 'By that time, not only had I come to the conclusion that I was going to have to confront the two of you together if I didn't want to risk being fobbed off with more deception, but I'd also remembered how that chemistry, that physical chemistry between you and I, could get sparked into passionate life at any given instant. You, as I then knew, were most of what you appeared more naturally to be. I remembered your natural look of being pleased to see me that time in the garden. I,' he confessed, 'started to hope.'

Willow raised her face to his and tenderly they kissed. As if they could never have enough of each other, in no time the physical chemistry between them had again sparked into passion.

Her cheeks were again flushed with wanting when, gently, Ryden put some space between them and, as if trying to cool the atmosphere, he lovingly teased, 'In a car? And you with a knee which I'm sure any good doctor will tell you is not ready for such antics?'

'It's—er—your fault,' Willow laughed.

'Which reminds me,' he murmured, 'you said something of the same sort once before.' His look had become serious. 'Are you now ready to put my mind permanently at rest about you and my brother? What, my darling, will you tell me,' he asked, 'is Noel—to you?'

'I'm hoping that he'll become a very dear brother, to me,' Willow quickly told him, her senses alert that Ryden still felt some inner disquiet on the subject of her and his brother. 'At the moment though, he's a man who, up until the morning of the Monday he flew to Paris to attend some computer exhibition to have talks with a Monsieur Ducret, I didn't know from Adam. He . . .'

'You didn't know Noel *until then*!' Ryden's exclamation cut across what she was saying. And, his brain obviously as active as ever he exclaimed, 'That must have been *after* that Gypsy female had told him, in no uncertain terms, to get lost?'

'It was,' Willow nodded. 'Noel was in his car. He'd been drowning his sorrows and had skidded off the road. Unfortunately, in doing so, he had managed to churn up the much cherished village green at Stanton Verney.' She saw from his eyes that Ryden had remembered his father referring to the report in the local paper of how the Stanton Verney village green zealots were on the warpath. 'I was out for an early morning jog when I saw what Noel's car had done to the green,' she went on. 'To be honest, I almost left him to his fate, but . . .'

'But you didn't?' Ryden asked, the tender look of adoration on his face for her making her heart beat erratically.

'I'd had a kindness shown to me on the previous Friday when my car had broken down,' she said. 'I passed the kindness on to Noel when I moved him over and drove his car into my garage.'

'He was incapable of driving!'

Willow hesitated to reveal how drunk Noel had been. But there had been too many deceptions between her and Ryden, so she told him, 'There was an empty Scotch bottle on the seat beside him—Noel didn't know until much later so much as what day of the week it was. Anyway,' she continued swiftly, 'when he did start to come round, he told me all about how disastrously his proposal to Gypsy had turned out, and—believing we were ships that pass in the night—I told him how I'd been going to go away on holiday, but how to have my car repaired was going to clear me out of cash. Anyhow,' she pressed on, 'Noel offered me the use of what I thought then was half his flat, to holiday in London, but I refused . . .'

'You refused!'

She nodded, then said, 'It wasn't until after Noel had gone, that I found he'd left behind a note stating the address of the flat, asking me to accept and saying that kindnesses were made to be passed on. He—er—also left behind the flat key. Two days later—I changed my mind, and used it.'

'Oh God,' groaned Ryden. 'To think, when I should have been fêting you for your kind hearted generosity to my brother, all I did was to snap and snarl, and try to throw you out!'

'You didn't know,' said Willow gently and reached up to kiss him.

'I didn't know,' he said gripping on to her fiercely, 'because I was too pig-headed to let you tell me.'

'I should have tried again,' she said, trying to take some of his anguish away. 'I was all set to when, at Broadhurst, I discovered that I loved you.'

'Oh, darling, why didn't you?' he asked and answering for her, 'I wasn't very approachable—was I?'

'It wasn't that,' she confessed. 'I'd made up my mind that when you came back from taking your father for a drive, that I'd have another try. Only, by the time you returned, Noel had come home.'

'Noel asked you to keep quiet?' Ryden asked, not sounding too pleased.

'He was appalled when first I told him about the mix up,' Willow told him hurriedly, 'and was all for coming to tell you himself. But, he'd 'phoned Gypsy from France, and had a date with her for the next evening. Suddenly, he was over-reacting—well, you know the way he feels about her,' she inserted by way of explanation. 'I suppose though,' she had to confess, 'that I revealed a little too much of how—er—none too—er—charming, you'd been with me. He became extremely agitated in fear that if you went for the real Gypsy the way you'd gone for me, that she would say goodbye to him for good and that he might never see her again. I'd just promised I'd keep quiet, about me not being Gypsy, when you came into the room with your father.'

With a hoarse, 'Come here,' Ryden hauled her close

up against his heart. 'God help me, my dearest love, that I should ever treat you so vilely . . .' Words choked him, and without saying anything else, he just held her close.

For how long then the rest of the world went by, Willow in her utter contentment to be in his arms, neither knew nor cared. But, at last, his tight hold on her relaxed and Ryden bestowed a brief but loving kiss to her mouth.

'Before I could chase after you when you belted out as if the house was on fire, I had to untangle myself from Noel—who must have thought when he tried to stop me, that I meant to harm you. Then I had to hare back in and wrest his car keys from him. While I want you completely and solely to myself, I also want to shout it from the roof tops that you have agreed to be mine. Shall we, my darling,' he asked, 'go back and tell everyone that I want only to love you and never, ever harm you and announce that very soon there is to be a wedding?'

'I'd—like that,' Willow smiled, and basked in Ryden's answering grin.

'Good—despite my lie about bringing you to Broadhurst for a cup of coffee, your future mother-in-law would dearly like to see you.'

Willow's heart was full to overflowing when Ryden turned his car around. 'What about Noel's car?' she asked as she spotted the car Ryden had used in his chase after her. 'Shall I drive it back?'

Cheerfully, Ryden drove past it. 'No way,' he said, 'While I can fully understand now the lengths one is driven to in the desperation of love, after what, through him, I've been made to endure, that young brother of mine can come and get it himself. Besides,' he added, quite capable of driving with one hand as his other hand sought and found hers, 'I don't want you anywhere but right here by my side for the rest of today—and for ever—after that.'

Willow smiled. Right by his side was the only place she wanted to be.

ROMANCE

Variety is the spice of romance

Each month, Mills & Boon publish new romances. New stories about people falling in love. A world of variety in romance — from the best writers in the romantic world. Choose from these titles in April.

SOME SAY LOVE Lindsay Armstrong
CAPTIVES OF THE PAST Robyn Donald
CAPABLE OF FEELING Penny Jordan
THE PLUMED SERPENT Annabel Murray
A GIRL NAMED ROSE Betty Neels
BEYOND REACH Margaret Pargeter
A RISKY BUSINESS Sandra K. Rhoades
MISLEADING ENCOUNTER Jessica Steele
GAME OF HAZARD Kate Walker
LIKE ENEMIES Sophie Weston
***THE RIGHT TIME** Maura McGiveny
***THE TIGER'S CAGE** Margaret Way

On sale where you buy paperbacks. If you require further information or have any difficulty obtaining them, write to: Mills & Boon Reader Service, PO Box 236, Thornton Road, Croydon, Surrey CR9 3RU, England.

*These two titles are available *only* from Mills & Boon Reader Service.

Mills & Boon

the rose of romance

CLAIRE HARRISON
Wild Flower